SLAY KING

THE GEORGIA SMOKE SERIES

NEW YORK TIMES BESTSELLING AUTHOR

ABBI GLINES

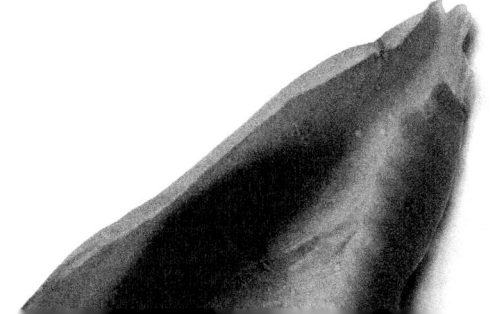

Slay
The Georgia Smoke Series
Copyright © 2024 by Abbi Glines
All rights reserved.
Visit my website at https://abbiglinesbooks.com

Cover Designer: Sarah Sentz, Enchanting Romance Designs
Editor: Jovana Shirley, Unforeseen Editing
www.unforeseenediting.com
Formatting: Melissa Stevens, The Illustrated Author
www.theillustratedauthor.com

• THE FAMILY •

*started by Jediah Hughes. It began with horse racing, moonshine,
and illegal arms in the early 1900s*

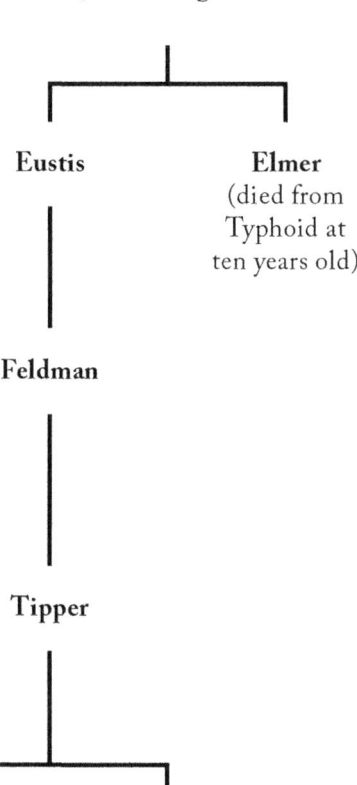

Jediah Hughes

Eustis

Elmer
(died from
Typhoid at
ten years old)

Feldman

Tipper

Garrett

Gregory
(died at three
years old in a
house fire)

• THE HUGHES •
Hughes Farm

Garrett Hughes (BOSS in books 1-9)
Wife: **Fawn Parker Hughes** → *SCORCH*

Blaise Hughes (Current BOSS/oldest son)
Wife: **Madeline Walsh Hughes** (parents Etta
Marks/dead and Liam Walsh/President of
Judgment MC)

Trev Hughes
Fiancée: **Gypsi
Parker** (also
stepsister) →
FIRECRACKER

Cree Elias Hughes →
SMOKESHOW and *FIREBALL*

• THE SHEPHERDS •
Oldest family inside the southern mafia other than the Hughes

Charles Livingston Shepherd
Best friend of Jediah Hughes

Gerald

Joseph
(became a priest)

Jeffrey
(died from Spanish
influenza at
fifteen years old)

Charles II

Darwin
(died from gunshot
at twenty-four)

Charles III
(drowned in
childhood)

Joshua
(became a
missionary)

Lincoln

Lincoln II (Linc)

Stellan

Mississippi Branch

Linc Shepherd
(left Florida to run Mississippi Branch when **Levi** was twenty-two)

Florida Branch

Levi Shepherd
Wife: **Aspen Chance Shepherd**→ *WHISKEY SMOKE*

Georgia Branch
Shepherd Ranch

Stellan Shepherd
Wife: **Mandilyn Shepherd**

Thatcher
→ *DEMONS July 2024* and
THATCHER'S DEMONS
August 2024

Sebastian
2 books coming
Fall 2024

· THE KINGSTONS ·
Mars Kingston joined the family in 1921

Mars Kingston
Childhood friend of Jediah Hughes

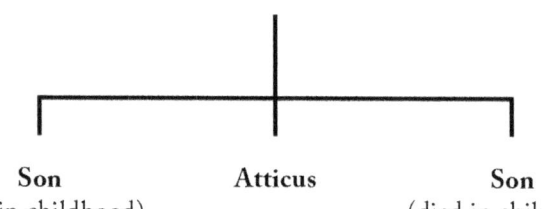

Hollis

Son
(died in childhood)

Atticus

Son
(died in childhood)

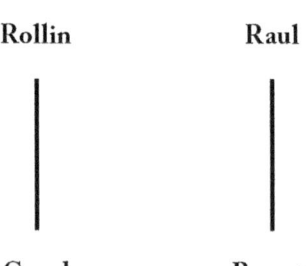

Rollin

Raul

Creed

Barrett

Florida Branch

Creed Kingston (dead)
Wife: **Abigail Kingston** (dead)

Huck
Wife: **Trinity Bennett Kingston**
→ *SMOKE BOMB*

Hayes (dead)
engaged to **Trinity** at
his death

Georgia Branch

Barrett Kingston
Wife: **Annette Kingston**

Storm
→ *SIZZLING May
2024* and *STORM
June 2024*

Lela
*Book coming in
2025*

Nailyah
*Book coming in
2025*

· THE HOUSTONS ·
Joined the family through horse racing in 1938

Kenneth Houston Wife: **Melanie Houston**
Moses Mile Ranch

Saxon Houston
Wife: **Haisley Slate Houston** →
SMOKIN' HOT

Winter Noel Houston

• THE LEVINES •
Joined the family in 1977

Alister Levine

|

Mississippi Branch

Luther Levine
Ex-Wife: **Chloe Wall**
(Moved from Florida when **Kye** was nineteen)

|

Florida Branch

Kye Levine
Wife: **Genesis Stoll Levine** → *BURN*

|

Jagger Henley Levine

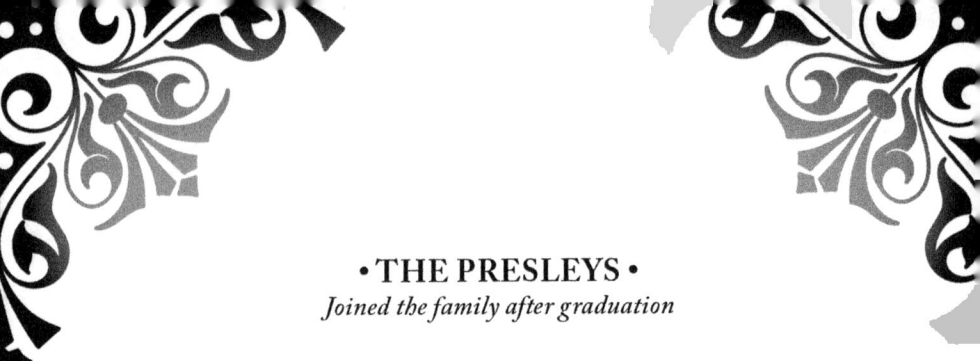

• THE PRESLEYS •
Joined the family after graduation

Gage Presley
Best friend of Blaise Hughes in high school
Wife: **Shiloh Carmichael Presley** → *STRAIGHT FIRE*

• THE SALAZARS •

Joined the family through horse racing in 1958

Georgia Branch only

Efrain Salazar

|

Gabriel Salazar (dead)
Wife: **Maeme Salazar**

|

Ex-Wife: **Estela Salazar** —— **Ronan Salazar** —— Wife: **Jupiter Salazar**

| |

King Salazar
→ *SLAY March 27, 2024* and
SLAY KING April 14, 2024   **Birdie**

· THE JONES ·

Joined the family through joined real-estate in 1966

Georgia Branch only

Hoyt Jones

Monte
Fiancée: **Bay Mintley**

Roland
Wife: **Luella Jones**

Wilder Jones
Wife: **Oakley Watson Jones**
→*ASHES*

Wells Jones
Book date coming
soon

Teller Jones
Book coming in
2025

Sarah Jones

· ACKNOWLEDGMENTS ·

Britt is always the first I mention. Without him, I would be insane. When I decided to write and release a book a month, he stood behind me. Believing in me and helping me run this house equally. We are a good team. He probably didn't realize I wasn't going to stop this crazy schedule anytime soon.

Emerson—because she is the one kid at home and the one affected by my writing schedule the most. But don't feel bad for her. She will not be ignored. Even if I tried. She makes sure to get her time in with me. As I edit this she's currently sleeping beside me on a plane headed to Paris. She'll survive.

My older children and granddaughter, who live in other states. They understand when they call or text and don't hear back from me for ten hours or so. If I am locked away, writing, they don't bother me until I let them know I am free. That's a lie. Ava doesn't give a shit if I am writing. If she wants to text me about what she did the night before or tell me about the coffee she is drinking that morning, she's texting me. And texting me. Until I respond.

My editor, Jovana Shirley at Unforeseen Editing, for always working with my crazy schedules and making my stories the best they can be. This has been a crazy ten months, and she has been brilliant. I appreciate her immensely.

My formatter, Melissa Stevens at The Illustrated Author. She makes my books beautiful inside. Her work is hands down the best formatting I've ever had in my books. I am always excited to see what she does with each one. Each book seems to be better than the last! It's amazing.

Autumn Gantz at Wordsmith Publicity, for saving me from losing my mind and taking over all the things that I can't keep up with anymore. Her help allows me to write more. Send her cookies.

Sarah Sentz, Enchanting Romance Designs for this badass cover.

Beta readers, who come through every time—Jerilyn Martinez and Vicci Kaighan. I love y'all!

Abbi's Army, for being my support and cheering me on. I love y'all!

My readers, for allowing me to write books. Without you, this wouldn't be possible.

•

To every broken heart
that has found healing
within the pages of a book.

•

• ONE •

Craving a man wasn't smart. Ever.

RUMOR

When one made rules, drew boundaries, protected themselves from situations that could cause damage, it must be something they stood firm on. That they demanded others respect. Showing weakness made those rules and boundaries seem like suggestions instead of guidelines.

King Salazar made it very difficult to remember why I had set the rules. He was the cause of them, yet every time he tried to push too far, I found myself unable to stop drawing closer to the flame. Craving a man wasn't smart. Ever.

Especially a man who had lied to you and manipulated you. Yet that was where I stood at the moment. Wanting what I shouldn't have. Wishing it were something it would never be.

I sat on the bed in the cottage that was located on the back of Maeme's property and listened to the silence around me. I'd been back in this house and out of King's bed for two weeks. Every night, King showed up with dinner. Talked to me as if we were friends, and we often watched television. Then, when I went to bed, he slept on the sofa. He refused to let me stay here at night alone. He didn't believe it was safe yet.

I didn't know who or what to believe.

What I did know was that I was a widow and I wasn't sad about it. My husband had been hell-bent on eventually beating me to death. King had made it possible for me to escape that life. It was one of the reasons I struggled with my feelings for him. Part of me felt as if I owed him. Another part held a slight worshipful reverence for him. It was messed up, but it was my truth. If he and the others hadn't come after Hill, the man I had made the mistake of marrying, then I'd still be there, being beaten. Or dead.

I also knew that I was willingly living under the protection of the Southern Mafia family. The sweet grandmother who had brought me in, given me a roof over my head, a sanctuary, was also part of the Mafia, just like King, her grandson.

Lastly, I was aware that there was a gang who wanted me for information on my dead husband. Which I did not have. Hill had never told me anything about his life. I knew nothing of his work or illegal activities.

So, I was here. This was the only safe place for me. Living in a storybook cottage with no bills. I'd stopped feeling guilty for being here. I no longer thought I was taking advantage of a nice lady's hospitality. They'd brought me here. I lived in this house because of their manipulation and planning. It shed a new light on the situation.

The door to the cottage opened, and I heard the screen slam shut. Standing up quickly, I stood there, frozen, listening. The only person who walked in without knocking was King, and he'd been gone when I woke up this morning. His pillow and blanket in a neat, folded pile on the end of the sofa.

"It's me," his familiar voice called out.

Sighing in relief, I made my way to the door that led into the living room just as he walked into it from the kitchen. My eyes locked on him, and the way my stomach fluttered at the sight of him frustrated me to no end. I didn't want to feel these things for him. I needed to protect my heart. But he made that so incredibly difficult.

The sexy smile that spread across his face didn't help matters. My chest joined my stomach at its fluttery mess of feelings.

"Morning, sweets," he drawled. "Sleep good?"

Yes, and no. Once I'd finally gotten to sleep and stopped fantasizing about him, then, yes, I'd slept well. It'd just taken me two hours for that to happen. Knowing he was asleep on my sofa, wearing nothing but a pair of boxer briefs, had been a distraction.

I simply nodded.

"Good," he replied, closing the space between us. He reached out and wrapped one of my curls around his fingers. "Damn, I like the way you look when you get up in the morning."

Hello, area between my legs. It was now wide awake with my stomach and chest. On high alert that the traitorous, lying man in front of me was close. Touching me. Making me want things.

"What are you doing back?" I asked, wishing I hadn't sounded breathless.

He didn't respond right away. Instead, he continued to play with my hair. I should move away. I had rules, and this was breaking one of those rules.

"I came to get you. Take you to breakfast at Maeme's," he replied finally.

Do not react. Do not melt. Stand firm.

"We had Sunday breakfast there three days ago," I replied.

The first time I had been back for Sunday breakfast after knowing the truth was interesting. Finding a way to associate the Mafia and these people I had come to care for was easier than I had thought it would be.

Having morals and realizing that your loyalty could shake the ground on which you'd thought you stood firm wasn't an easy pill to swallow. It was a reevaluation of yourself. What you had become. What made you who you were. Your core.

"This isn't a family event," he said as my curl slid from his fingers.

"Then, what is it?"

He slipped a finger under my chin. "It's Maeme wanting to check on you."

She worried about me more than anyone ever had. One of those things that nagged at me. I had known many people in my life. I had been placed in different homes. Had to trust strangers. Never had I trusted any of them the same way I did Maeme. With her, I truly felt that she cared. She wanted me safe.

It seemed unfair. Why couldn't I overlook the bad with King? Trust him like I did her. They were the same essentially. They were a part of this dark underworld thing. She'd lied to me just like he had.

I hadn't slept with her. I hadn't fallen in love with her. It made a monumental difference. One I could not control. One I wished I had power over.

"She doesn't have to feed me for that," I replied.

King took another strand of hair between his fingers and chuckled. "I'll let you tell her that."

He knew I would never do such a thing. I said nothing in return as I stood there.

"Come on, sweets. You know you want to go spend hours in the library."

That was true. Maeme's library was full of books I wanted to get lost in.

"So, you're not staying?" I asked him. Unsure what I wanted the answer to be.

"No, I'm not. I've got somewhere to be," he replied. "But I'll be back tonight. I'll bring tacos."

He'd be back. Just hearing him say it made my mood improve.

"I need to get dressed," I said, moving back away from him. "I won't be long."

The last thing I saw before I spun around to rush back into the bedroom was the amused gleam in his eyes. He knew I was weak. His coming every night was him trying to break me down. Win my forgiveness and regain my trust. And I wanted him there. Another one of my problems, but at least I was willing to admit it. I wasn't lying to myself. Someone had to be honest with me. Might as well *be me*.

If he was here, then he wasn't with another woman. But then I already knew he'd taken a woman to the tack room two weeks ago. I'd had the unfortunate experience of hearing them in there. Was that something I could handle, knowing if he did it again? I didn't feel as if I could ask or if I could even be angry if he chose to. I had drawn a line, and I was the one enforcing it. He was free to do as he pleased with anyone else. Although the idea crushed me.

My mood instantly sank again as I put on a pair of shorts, a blouse, and my sandals. King was a very sexual man. He had his kinks, and he was used to women throwing themselves at him. Just because he was coming here to babysit me at night didn't mean he wasn't tying up some female in the tack room and doing those things to her before he screwed her.

"Give me a grocery list, and I'll go grab what you want today," King called from the other room.

I glanced at myself in the mirror. I'd forgotten what it was like to go without makeup. When I'd been married to Hill, I'd had to cover up the bruises so often, and he believed I was being lazy if I didn't put it on every day. I brushed my fingers over my cheekbone. The smooth, unmarked skin reminded me what all I had been given here.

They had lied to me. But they had also saved me. The reflection staring back at me wasn't the same trusting, wide-eyed girl I had been before marrying Hill. There was a darkness in my eyes that time had placed there. Betrayal had stolen so much from me. A large part of who I was had been snatched away.

Not by the people who have given me somewhere safe, but by the man I had married. All Hill had ever done to me was take from me. Hurt me. Steal any cause for happiness.

King had lied to me, but he'd never hurt me. Being around him made me happy even if I didn't want it to. Letting myself love him was a mistake, but it was already done. I just didn't know where we went from here or how.

"Rumor?" he said as he walked into the room. My gaze swung from the mirror to him standing just inside the doorframe. "You good?"

The grocery list. I'd forgotten he'd said that.

I smiled and nodded. "I'm fine," I replied, then turned to pick up my purse.

"Damn, you sure are filling out a pair of shorts real nice. I like your ass with that bubble to it."

I narrowed my eyes and glared at him. "Are you saying my butt is getting fat?"

King walked over to me, and I took one step back, not sure I trusted myself to get close again and not bury my nose in his shirt.

"I'm saying, I like you eating properly. Your body is always sexy as fuck, sweets. But with the new curves, it's damn near poetic."

"Poetic?" I asked.

His hand slid over my hip. "The kind of dips and swells that inspire the greatest of poetry." Then, he squeezed the undeniable extra plump that had been added to my bottom, thanks to Maeme's cooking. "I'd kill whoever you asked me to if I could watch this sweet ass bounce while I was spanking it."

Oh good Lord. I took a deep, steadying breath. *Stay focused.*

We needed to go to Maeme's. He had things to do. Later, while alone, I'd live that little fantasy out in my head while getting some relief.

"We should go," I blurted out.

"I'd kiss it real nice," King said in a husky whisper, pulling me up against him. "But I'd bite it first. Make you scream out. Then, I'd lick it."

I closed my eyes and sucked in a deep gulp of oxygen. "Stop!" I demanded in a strangled voice.

King let out a low groan before dropping his hand and stepping back. He looked at me through hooded lids, and the hunger flashing in his blue eyes made me tremble. With a lift of his hands, he moved farther away from me.

"I'll wait out in the truck," he said in a raspy voice before leaving me there alone. With my own racing heart and an ache between my legs.

· TWO ·

I wasn't sure if the fact that I was mesmerized by him in this moment meant I was mentally unstable or if it was an unavoidable occurrence.

RUMOR

Inside the truck, King was quiet, and I spent the short drive to Maeme's house trying to think of something to say. When he pulled up beside the expensive-looking sports car parked outside, his jaw clenched, and I watched him, unsure if I should be concerned. I glanced around the yard, but saw nothing out of the ordinary.

King swung the door open to his truck with a hard push, then stepped out. He was angry about something, but I didn't think I was the cause of it. By the time I climbed out of the truck, King was in front of me. I stared up at him, trying to figure out what had upset him.

"Don't let Sebastian touch you," King said, crowding me back against the passenger door.

"What?" I asked, confused.

King lowered his head as his eyes held mine. "Don't let him touch you. Keep your distance."

I glanced over at the car. It didn't look like one of the cars I'd seen in Sebastian's garage, but I assumed it must be his. "Sebastian is my friend," I said, finally looking back at him.

King's hand shot out, and he grabbed my chin. "Don't test me, Rumor."

I wasn't sure if the fact that I was mesmerized by him in this moment meant I was mentally unstable or if it was an unavoidable occurrence.

"Fine," I breathed. "I won't let him touch me."

King studied me hard, as if trying to read my thoughts and make sure I meant what I had said before releasing me. "Good girl."

And there were those two words that, when used by King, made me want to melt at his feet. Words I wasn't familiar with. Praise was something I had never experienced in my life. Clearly, I craved it. When King did it, every nerve ending in my body felt as if they had been given a jolt of pleasure.

He straightened, then put his hand possessively on my back. I let him lead me to the house and even open the door for me to go inside. The way he seemed to be strung up tight still was odd. It wasn't as if my being around Sebastian had bothered him like this before.

Voices carried through the house from the dining room. The sound of female laughter that was not Maeme's surprised me. I felt King's hand flinch where he was touching me.

Before I could ask who was here, a tall, willowy blonde stepped into the hallway. Her eyes barely grazed me, but they lit up like fireworks when she locked them on King. The wide, perfectly straight white smile that appeared on her face made my stomach feel sick.

"KING!" she squealed loudly, then rushed toward him.

His hand left my back just in time for him to catch her as she wrapped her arms around him. I stared at their bodies embracing. He was touching her, yet I wasn't supposed to touch Sebastian. Maybe she was another relative.

"Scotlin," he replied, but his smile appeared forced.

"It's been a year. That should be illegal. We've never gone that long without seeing each other," she replied and then inhaled his shirt before tilting her head back to gaze up at him.

A relative wouldn't have just sniffed him. Not like that.

"You're finally here," Sebastian drawled as he entered the now-crowded hallway. "We need to go."

The woman patted King's cheek. "It's been too long since we worked together. This is gonna be fun."

Sebastian flashed me a sympathetic smile as I tried to figure this all out.

"Yeah," King replied, disentangling himself from her limbs that seemed to cling to him everywhere. "We need to head out."

I watched as he turned his back on the other woman and gave me his full attention.

"I'll see you tonight," he said.

I nodded. It wasn't like I could ask who she was since he wasn't introducing me. That was a red flag. A big, huge one. But then I had made the rules and drawn lines for a reason. I didn't trust King. We were not in a relationship. Which was why I shouldn't have agreed to not touch Sebastian. I hadn't been planning on it, of course, but that wasn't the point.

He reached up and cupped my face. "Stay here today. Enjoy the library."

Again, I just nodded.

"I'm riding with you. Sebastian can take my car," the woman stated, once again wrapping her arms around a part of King. This time, it was his arm, and then she tugged him.

He ignored her as he waited for me to say something.

"Okay," I replied, dropping my eyes to the ground. I didn't want to look at him or whoever the woman was pulling on him.

"Call me if you need anything," he urged.

"Oh my God, King. She has Maeme," the woman said, sounding exasperated.

King swung his eyes to her. "Stay the fuck out of this."

To my shock, she didn't even appear bothered. Instead, she grinned provocatively, then hissed at him before turning and strutting toward the front door.

"Go on now," Maeme said firmly.

King's gaze flickered over to his grandmother, then back to me.

Not even able to force a smile, I stepped away from him, then headed in Maeme's direction. When I reached her, she put an arm around me and walked me into the kitchen. Not looking back was hard, but I managed it. Mostly because I didn't want Maeme to catch me.

The stack of waffles didn't distract me from the swirl of jealousy, insecurity, and hurt that only King seemed to inspire.

"Her name is Scotlin May. She was literally the girl next door for King, growing up. Her family isn't a part of us, but we work together. Her father is a state representative and will eventually be governor because of the pull we have. That's all I can share without it being gossip. But that frown on your pretty face, let that go. Scotlin has no hold on King. He has a soft spot for her because of their past, but nothing more. Doesn't seem to keep her from trying though. Never has."

Nothing she had just said made me feel any better. Quite possibly, I felt worse. "She's … Jefferson May's daughter?"

Everyone in Georgia knew he was running for governor in the next election. He pushed family values and religion, and the South loved him.

"Yes. And it will benefit us particularly to have the new governor in our pocket. We have some control over our current one, but not to the extent the family wields over the governors of Florida, Alabama, Mississippi, and Tennessee. We need that kind of power here too."

And so Scotlin May was important to them. I didn't like it. I was pretty sure I hated it. First, there were the women who looked like porn stars and let King whip them in the tack room. Now, I had to deal with someone like Scotlin May in his life.

"Come eat," she said, making her way to the island, where the food was spread out like a buffet.

Not having an appetite wasn't going to be a good enough excuse for Maeme. I had to make myself eat. My thoughts went to Scotlin May's tall, thin body. She looked lost here, as if she were supposed to be on a runway somewhere in Paris but took a wrong turn and ended up in Madison. I bet she didn't eat waffles. Hill would call me fat, if he were alive. I hadn't weighed myself since arriving here because it had been a prison I wanted to escape. The power he held over me. The way it mocked me if I ate something I shouldn't have. Hill would beat me. Curse at me about being lazy and not taking care of my body. He had wanted a wife who looked like Scotlin May.

I took the plate from Maeme and placed a singular waffle and a spoonful of berries onto it before taking the maple syrup and lightly drizzling it over the top.

"I know King said he'd be back tonight, but that was wishful thinking. He knows not to promise such. Why don't you stay here with me? You can sleep in the blue room."

Would he have lied to me about that? Why not tell me the truth? He had promised not to lie to me anymore, but then did that mean anything really? Would I ever know if he was telling me the truth?

"Do you think it's still unsafe for me to stay alone?" I asked her.

She nodded her head. "Yeah. It's why King has been staying at the house with you instead of going back to his place or the room in the stables."

That was the first time I'd heard someone talk about his place. I knew he said he stayed at the stables most of the time, but I hadn't realized he had a home somewhere else. Was it an apartment? I doubted it was a house. He was a single man who barely lived there.

I realized Maeme was watching me. Waiting for a response.

"Oh, uh, thank you. I'll stay if you think it's best."

"Yes, it is best. Now, tell me, how are you feeling? I'm happy you chose to stay with us, but are you still good with that decision?"

I set my plate down, then climbed up and sat on the barstool before responding, "Yes, I think I made the right choice." That was a lie. I wasn't at all sure that I had. I just didn't think I had the strength to walk away from him. The thought was more painful than the betrayal had been.

"You're gonna be fine. Soon, you'll have a life again. One where you can go to the store and feel safe. You can do whatever you want. Start over fresh."

I stared down at the food on my plate. "I don't even have a college degree," I told her.

"You have plenty of money to get one of those if you want. When the time is right," she said with a pat on my back.

I shook my head. "I don't have any money," I replied.

Hill had never given me access to his accounts.

"Of course you do. It's all safely tucked away for now until this mess is over with the Insantos gang. It's been hidden for you and will be given to you when the time comes."

I shook my head, not understanding. "What do you mean?"

Maeme squeezed my hand with one of hers. "The bastard you were married to. We got back what he'd stolen from us, and then the rest was placed away for you. He's dead. You were his wife. The money belongs to you. Then, there will be the money from the sale of your house. King is overseeing that."

I was speechless. The house itself would sell for almost two million dollars. I knew he hadn't owned it, and there was a mortgage, but he had bragged about what a good investment it was. It was worth half a million more than what he'd originally paid for it.

"That's ... that's a lot of money," I said, trying to wrap my head around it.

"That it is, my dear. Your future looks bright. I can't wait to see you flourish. Spread your wings. Live the life you deserve."

What did that even mean, the life I deserved?

· THREE ·

You'll release dark shit.

RUMOR

The warmth of the body covering my back woke me. I opened my mouth to scream when a large hand muffled the sound.

"Easy, sweets. It's just me," King's deep voice said close to my ear.

I stared at the wall, trying to decide if this was a dream or real. King didn't get in my bed anymore. He obeyed the rules and lines I had set. Even when I lay in bed at night with him in the other room, wishing he would defy them and come to me.

"I'm gonna remove my hand, but don't scream. Or Maeme will be in here with her Glock pointed at my head within seconds."

I nodded as his hand left my mouth to caress my arm.

"Good girl," he praised as if I had done something worthy of it.

"What are you doing in here?" I asked quietly.

He pressed a kiss to my shoulder. "You're here," he replied as he left another kiss on my neck.

I closed my eyes and attempted to will my body not to react. Which was a joke.

"You … you're in bed with me." My words came out as a stammer while he nuzzled against me.

"Mmhmm," he murmured. "And you feel like heaven. I've missed you."

This wasn't fair. All my good intentions seemed weak when tested. King's body, his scent …

I gasped as he pressed his erection against my bottom. Nope, not fair.

"I know there are rules and lines," he said against my skin as he brushed his lips close to my collarbone. "But I need you, sweets. It was a real fucking bad day, and I need to be reminded of the good. The exceptional. Please."

I sucked in a deep breath and tried not to tremble when his hand cupped my breast.

"Just give me tonight. I need you." The pleading in his tone was close to desperation.

What had happened that shook him like this? And how was I supposed to tell him no? I couldn't when he sounded so vulnerable.

Slowly, I rolled over onto my back and stared up at him as he hovered over me. Those blue eyes searched my face. The haunted look that gazed back at me was my undoing. I reached up and cupped the side of his stubbled jaw.

What had happened today?

His eyes closed briefly, and he leaned into my touch. Lines were about to be blurred. I had set them in place to protect myself, but right now, all I cared about was helping him. Fixing whatever was wrong. Gone was the woman who had questioned his intentions. He was able to make me forget so easily.

No words seemed to be needed. It was as if he was reading my thoughts. The relief in his eyes was overpowered immediately by the man. The one who wanted me. The one who made me feel things I'd never known were possible. I had gone to sleep tonight, jealous. Of the woman he was with. I had even imagined that they would sleep together tonight. But he was here. With me.

King moved over me then. His knees on either side of my legs. I lifted my hips as he slid my panties down to my ankles, then tossed them aside. "Open your legs." His tone was commanding, even in a hoarse whisper.

The intensity of his focus as I did as I had been told made me shiver. I'd missed this too. Being with him. How he made me feel.

"I want your pussy leaking with my cum again."

A whimper escaped me as he stood up and discarded his boxers. His eyes never leaving my body. The way he looked at me made me feel as if I were the most beautiful woman on earth. While I knew that wasn't the case, when I was with King, I almost believed it.

"Can you be quiet?" he asked, lowering himself over me.

I wasn't sure. I blinked up at him, and he grinned.

"It's okay, sweets. I'll cover your mouth if you need to be loud. You can even bite my hand."

I opened my mouth to say something, but whatever it was slipped my thoughts as King filled me with one hard thrust. His hand clamped down over my mouth firmly to muffle the cry that tore from me.

"FUUUCK," he groaned near my ear, then rocked his hips and did it again.

My body bucked beneath him from the sharp sting of being stretched.

"You take my dick like such a good girl," he snarled.

I lifted my gaze from his biceps flexing as he held himself up enough so that I could breathe to meet his eyes. There was a sinister gleam in them that shouldn't excite me, but it did. Although I was completely willing, the way his blue eyes darkened as he held me down, muffling me, was thrilling.

He eased back slowly, then shoved deep inside me again, throwing his head back, displaying the veins standing out on his neck. I was mesmerized by the sheer beauty.

When his eyes met mine again, he gave me a wicked grin. "Fight me," he said.

Fight him? What did he mean?

He moved his hand from my face and ran a finger over my bottom lip. "I want you to fight me, sweets. While I fuck you, bite me. Hit me. Get out all the anger, hurt, everything you've pent up. Take it out on me while I sink into you over and over."

I stared at him. He wanted me to hurt him? I shook my head.

His hand fisted in my hair and tugged my head back until my neck was bare to him. "Every time you felt helpless, scared, terrified, and didn't have the strength to fight back, do it now. Use me to get it out."

A panicky tightness started in my chest. I didn't understand this. The things he was talking about were things that he hadn't caused. Why would he want me to use him to release that? And during sex?

"Why?" I choked out.

He jerked on my hair and lowered his face to my neck and licked it in one long motion. "It's therapeutic," he said, then licked me again. "You'll release dark shit," he whispered. "It'll make me come so fucking hard."

King continued licking me as he made his way down to my chest. I watched him while his reasons replayed in my head. Just as he was about to reach my nipple, I grabbed a handful of his hair and snatched his mouth away. His eyes flared brightly as they locked on mine.

Then … I slapped him. That beautiful face barely moved from the force, but the approval in his eyes only seemed to push me further. Grabbing his shoulders, I dug my nails into his skin.

King snapped into action then. He slammed back into me hard while his eyes blazed with a ferocity I'd never seen. I slapped him again, and the grin that spread across his face was almost evil. If he wasn't so stunningly perfect, it would have been terrifying.

"Keep on," he encouraged me as he licked his lips. "Hurt me."

He had set off some trigger inside me I hadn't known existed. I began to claw at him, shove him, hit his chest, as he pounded into me over and over. The spiral was closing in on me quickly, and if I wasn't so desperate for it, I would have tried to put it off for more of whatever this was we were doing.

"Harder!" I shouted, and his hand came over my mouth again.

"That's my little wildcat," he said, then bit his bottom lip hard.

I fought against his hand on my face, and his fingers flexed.

"You don't always have to be good," he told me. "You get to be bad too, sweets. You get to act out. Fight back."

My hand was wrapped around his wrist, but I stopped trying to take his hand from my mouth. While I stared up into his eyes, I felt my body ignite, then explode as I screamed against his palm.

"Fuck, baby," he grunted.

Then, his body jerked against me, and I felt it. The warmth. The heat rush into me. His hips pumped into me twice more as he let out a deep, low moan.

When his hand moved from my face to tangle into my hair, he rolled off me, pulling me with him until I was sprawled half on top of his chest. I could feel his heart racing against my cheek.

King ran his fingertips along my side as his breathing slowed, along with his heartbeat. "I missed being inside you," he said in a raspy voice.

I had missed it too. The connection. The feeling as if I'd found where I belong. Even after the lies, I'd ached for this. For what King could give me.

"I don't want the lines and rules," he said then. "I understand why you think you need them, but you don't. This, us, it was never a lie."

I let out a heavy sigh. "I want to believe that."

King shifted so that I was on my back on the mattress again and he was the one looking down at me. "It's the fucking truth," he said in a fierce tone, then reached for my right leg and pulled it back, opening me up to him. "That right there. My cum is leaking out of you. I don't do that, sweets. I don't come in women. But with you, I need to do it. I need to mark you. It's twisted, and I don't understand it, but I can't help it. This is why you can trust me."

I started to attempt to close my thighs, and he held me firmly open. His gaze flicked from me to between my legs a few times before he ran his knuckles over my tender flesh. I winced and trembled simultaneously.

"Nothing eases the shit in my chest like this does," he said just above a whisper. "Don't keep it from me. Let me have this back, you back."

As much as I wanted to give him whatever he asked for, I knew I had to be careful.

"What happens when you tire of me?" It was more vulnerable than I had ever been with him. Stating my fears aloud. It didn't go unnoticed. I realized that King did in fact have some of my trust.

"Sweets," he said as he slid a finger inside of me, "I can't imagine that day will come, but who is to say it won't be you who gets tired of me?"

There was a difference that I wasn't going to verbalize. I'd been as open with him as I could be. Telling him I was in love with him wasn't an option. If I wanted to get rid of him, I already knew that would be the way to send him running. I couldn't love enough for both of us.

"Fuck, that's slick," he murmured. "Spread them. I need more."

Unable to hold on to my good sense, I opened my legs for him again.

• F O U R •

And you're the goddamn Mafia.

K I N G

The biscuit I was about to put into my mouth was slapped out of my hand. My gaze collided with Maeme. She was not in grand-mother mode. She was in pissed-off Maeme mode. She didn't have to say a word. I already knew. She'd heard us. Damn. I had tried to keep it down, but then I'd also been unable to stay out of Rumor's tight cunt.

"What are you doing?" she hissed at me.

"Trying to eat a biscuit," I replied with a grin I hoped cooled off my heated grandmother.

She pointed her finger in my face. "That is not want I mean, and you know it."

I stepped back and leaned against the edge of the sink. "I'm not gonna be able to stay away from her." Might as well get that out there now. Nothing she was going to say could stop me.

"And what happens when she sees the news? Or someone says something to her about your engagement?" Maeme snapped.

Not what I wanted to dwell on this morning. I'd gotten my peace, buried deep inside Rumor last night. After an entire fucking day of having to set up a fictional relationship with Scotlin, I needed to have Rumor. She'd come to me so willingly, and, damn, it had eased all the shit in my head. Maeme reminding me about what had gone down yesterday wasn't helping me. I was going to end up back in bed with Rumor.

"I'll explain it to her," I bit out through clenched teeth. "It's not like it's real."

Maeme threw up her hands. "No one can know that."

"Rumor can know," I argued.

Although I wasn't entirely sure I was allowed to tell her. Blaise hadn't said anything about keeping it from Rumor.

"The more she knows, the more danger she will be in. You can't tell her anything. Her safety is supposed to be our only concern. Not your need to fuck her."

"Maeme," I began, but she slapped a hand on my chest, harder than necessary.

"I want that girl to have happiness. I want her to have the life she's never had. Don't get her messed up in this. She isn't strong enough for our world. We will protect her and make sure she has all she needs. But you?" She dug the tip of her nail into my chest. "You are going to mess around and break her heart."

Footsteps upstairs stopped me from what I was going to say. Rumor was awake.

I had come here last night, needing to wash away the fake kiss I'd had to give Scotlin while we pretended to be out on the town together. Making sure pictures were taken of us at every hot spot in Atlanta. With me touching her. Pretending with her. Having her hands all over me. The engagement had to seem real when it was announced. Once we called it a night, I wanted a shower and to get Scotlin's perfume off me. After that, I had been like a crazed man, needing a fix. Rumor being my fix.

"This could take months. You can't have Rumor behind closed doors and successfully sell your engagement to Scotlin in public. The Derby is in ten days, and you have to go on the arm of Scotlin May. The diamond ring has to be on her hand and flashed around for all to see. Jupiter has already started the planning for the engagement party being held at Barrett and Annette's in a month."

My ears were trained on the footsteps upstairs.

"I'm telling Rumor. No more lies with her," I repeated.

"You can't," she argued.

"Yes, I can."

Maeme stalked across the kitchen. "Your father can deal with it."

"I won't lose her," I said. "Try and understand that I need her."

Maeme spun around and glared at me. "You're being selfish."

Was I? It didn't feel selfish. It felt real. Like the most real thing in my life.

The footsteps faded, and I pointed to the ceiling to quiet Maeme. Rumor had walked out of her room and was probably headed to the stairs.

Maeme just shook her head and turned back to the cabinets and jerked one open.

I turned my gaze to the door, waiting on Rumor to appear. When she did, it was even better than I had anticipated. Her eyes swung to me, and the pink flush on her cheeks was so damn sweet that I wanted to toss her over my shoulder and take her back upstairs. The five-foot-tall woman currently pissed at me was the only reason I didn't.

"Morning," I said as I walked over to her.

The way she followed me with her eyes nervously but with a glint of pleasure had me forgetting the shit I was currently facing.

"Good morning," she replied softly.

I reached for her hand and wrapped it in mine. "You gotta be hungry. Come eat," I said, tugging her closer to me. "I'll fix your plate."

"Good Lord, let the woman breathe," Maeme scolded from behind me.

I winked at Rumor before sliding a hand to her back and turning to face Maeme. "I was just being a gentleman, Maeme."

My grandmother rolled her eyes and set the orange juice on the counter. "You have work to do. I'll get Rumor fed. You can go."

I had a meeting with the others at the Shephard Ranch. Blaise Hughes would be there on a video call. It wasn't a meeting I wanted to be at, but I was required. Since it was me they were forcing to be fake engaged to Scotlin. All to weed out her father's mole and to find out who had been leaving the notes on her car, stalking her. It was more than likely the same person, and the sooner he was found, the sooner I could stop pretending with Scotlin.

"I got twenty minutes," I replied, not looking in Maeme's direction.

"Go," Rumor told me. "Don't be late."

I wanted to tell her about Scotlin before I left, but with Maeme breathing down my neck, it wasn't going to be possible. I'd tell her tonight. Back at the cottage, where I wanted her. Not here with my grandmother making it difficult.

Leaning down, I pressed a kiss to Rumor's lips. "Be at the cottage this evening. I'll bring dinner," I whispered.

She nodded.

I'd talk to her then. This was all going to be fine.

"Glad you could join us," my father said, giving me a pointed look when I walked into Stellan Shephard's office.

"Maeme cooked breakfast," I replied with a shrug, taking a seat on the sofa beside Wilder and across from Thatcher, who was grinning at me, clearly not buying my excuse.

"It's true then?" Wilder asked beside me. "*You* have caught feelings for a woman? I thought they were talking shit."

I glanced at Wilder, willing him to shut the fuck up before looking at Stellan. "You want a recap on last night, or do I wait until the call with Blaise?"

Change of subject. Hopefully.

"You left Scotlin last night and went directly to Rumor," my father pointed out.

"I left her at my fucking house. Isn't that enough?"

Stellan leaned forward, resting his elbows on the desk. "Scotlin's safety is important."

No shit. "I'm aware of that, and my house is safe. Not to mention the security that her father has on her."

Stellan raised an eyebrow. "You are her security. The others are just there for looks."

"They're former Marines. One was a fucking sniper," I pointed out.

"And you're the goddamn Mafia!" my father shouted.

"Easy, Ronan," Barrett Kingston said to my father, holding up a hand to stop him. "King always gets the job done."

Thank you, Barrett!

"Yes, but before, he was never locked on a piece of ass," my father shot back.

I was standing before I knew it. My annoyance had morphed into a full-blown rage. "Don't," I warned him. "Don't call her that again."

Thatcher let out a deep, low chuckle. "To think I didn't want to come today. I'd have missed the fucking entertainment."

"Shut up, Thatch," Wilder told him.

"It's time to call Blaise," Stellan told the room. "This has to end. Now."

Fine by me.

"Why? It's his fucking fault. He's the one who told King to fuck her," Thatcher said as he lit up a cigarette. "Seems like his problem."

"Thatcher," Stellan warned his oldest son with a hard glare.

Thatcher took a long pull, then smirked in response. I'd love to agree with him, but I knew that even without Blaise's orders to make Rumor want to stay, it would have happened. The bomb had been ticking. I'd been slowly giving in to what I wanted. And what I wanted was Rumor.

The ringing immediately ended, and Blaise Hughes appeared on the flat screen that covered a large portion of the far wall.

"Before we get started, Thatcher, you need to call Huck. We got a hit that needs to happen in Atlanta before noon," Blaise said from where he was sitting behind his desk back in Ocala.

Thatcher stood up and put his cigarette out in the ashtray. "On it," he replied before heading to the door.

"Take backup if you think you need it," Blaise said.

"I don't." Thatcher smirked before opening the door and leaving.

"Storm, go with him," Stellan ordered.

We all knew it wasn't because he thought his oldest son needed backup. Sending Thatcher anywhere alone wasn't smart. His twisted head would do more than kill whoever it was that Blaise wanted dead. If left to his own devices, he'd leave them nailed to a damn wall or some crazy execution-style shit.

Blaise leaned back in his chair. "Let's get started."

· FIVE ·

You don't know that much about King, do you?

RUMOR

The knock on my door came at the same time my phone buzzed with a text. I never got messages from anyone other than King, so I grabbed it before going to see who was here. He wouldn't be knocking and texting me at the same time. Although it was almost eight at night and he still hadn't arrived.

Glancing down at my phone, I read:

I'm sorry. Things got complicated today, and I can't get there tonight. Maeme is going to get you, and you are staying with her.

The disappointment was instant as I slipped my phone into the pocket of my jean shorts and headed to the door to let Maeme inside. I shouldn't have slept with him last night. Being with him like that had made me want things I couldn't have. King wasn't a forever guy. We weren't in a real relationship. Yet I was feeling too deeply.

When I reached the front door, it wasn't Maeme. I unlocked the bolt and opened it while studying Sebastian through the window. His eyes met mine, and he smiled.

"Hey," he said simply.

"Hey," I replied, stepping back for him to come inside.

He walked past me and into the kitchen. "Man, it's been years since I've been in here."

"Really?" I asked. "Who lived here then?"

A deep chuckle came from him as he turned to look at me. "No one at the time, which is why I came here." He paused, and a crooked smile tugged at his lips. "It was a great place to bring a girl back in the day. Well, that is, until Maeme caught us doing it and changed the locks."

I laughed at the thought of Maeme catching them. "Great. I'm hoping the mattress has been replaced since then."

Sebastian's smile only grew. "None of us used the bed. We knew we couldn't make it look the way Maeme did, so we didn't go near it."

"The sofa?" I asked, raising my eyebrows, wondering what I would find with a blue light and not wanting to sit on it anymore.

"Eh," he said and walked toward the doorway that led into the living area. "Ah. You're safe. That is *not* the same sofa."

I let out a loud sigh. "That is the best news I have heard all day."

My phone dinged in my pocket, and I ignored it. King had sent me another text. I didn't want to answer him because I wouldn't lie if he asked me, and I knew telling him that Sebastian was here wouldn't go over well.

"Maeme sent me to get you. That's probably her or King letting you know he won't be back tonight and you need to go stay there."

I nodded. "Yeah, King already told me. I'll go grab my overnight bag." Thankfully, I hadn't unpacked since I'd gotten back today. I had been too excited about the new books I had to read from the library at Maeme's.

Once I got to my room, I pulled out the phone to read the newest text.

Rumor?

I replied so he would stop worrying.

I am getting my things together now.

After sending it, I grabbed the bag with my stuff and went back to the kitchen where Sebastian stood, looking out the window over the sink. His arms were crossed over his chest, and when he wasn't standing beside King, he seemed larger. It wasn't that he was a small man. He was over six feet tall at least, and his arms were corded with muscle. His long legs weren't as thick as Kings, but they still filled out a pair of jeans well. I wondered if riding horses was why they all seemed to have such nice butts.

He turned to look at me, and I realized he'd caught me staring. The grin that curled on his lips wasn't as cocky as King's, but it was a close second. I shook my head and let out a small laugh. They were all a little full of themselves.

Something hit me I hadn't thought of before.

"Do the women you all … bring around know what you are?" I asked him.

He ran his hand over his mouth as his smile spread, then nodded. "Yeah. Anyone we bring onto the property has had a thorough background check and been approved. They are given the rules and warned about what happens if they talk."

Interesting. But it made sense.

"What happened to Sedona?" I asked, realizing that with all I'd found out following her being threatened at the stables, I hadn't heard anything about her. My focus had been on me, on King, and on trying to figure out what we were doing.

Sebastian walked over to me and took my bag, and then his eyes locked on mine. "Do you really want those details?" The warning in his gaze was obvious.

I felt a coldness settle in my chest. Twisting as it sank in. I didn't want to ask now. He was right. I wasn't sure I wanted the details, but I also knew this would haunt me.

"Is she … dead?" My question came out in a whisper.

"No."

I let out a relieved sigh and placed my hand on my heart. "Thank God."

Sebastian smirked. "God's not the one that gets credit for that. I assure you. Those outside of the family refer to him as the Devil."

I wasn't sure I wanted to ask who that might be.

"Come on," Sebastian said. "Maeme's waiting."

I followed him outside and out to a truck. It was a fancy, expensive-looking one, but it was still a truck. I let out a small laugh at the sight of it.

"What's funny?" Sebastian asked me as he opened the passenger door.

I waved a hand at the vehicle. "This and you. I don't see you driving a truck. You're more of a Porsche guy."

He tossed my bag inside, then stepped back so I could climb inside. "A Porsche guy? Why is that? King drives a truck. How are we any different?"

I sat down and looked at him. "You live in a mansion. Have a dozen vehicles in your underground garage. There's a movie theater in your house. You're high-profile, expensive. You might ride horses, but you are not a country boy."

He tilted his head and shook it with an amused look on his face. "You don't know that much about King, do you?"

What was that supposed to mean? I frowned at him, suddenly wondering what it was I didn't know. I thought I knew him.

Sebastian rubbed his jaw for a minute, and I could see the indecision on his face. He was struggling with telling me things. But this was about King, and since I was having sex with him regularly and I'd fallen in love with him secretly, I kinda thought I should know the man.

"King has his own house. You know that, right?"

I nodded. Although I hadn't been aware it was a house. I had imagined more of an apartment.

Sebastian let out a groan. "Listen, this isn't my shit to share. But I will tell you that King grew up just like I did. Same kind of life. We are the same. More so than Wells or Wilder even." He paused a moment, then grabbed the door like he was going to close it. "But for the record, King has a fucking Jaguar."

I sat there, letting that sink in and trying to imagine it as Sebastian walked around the front of the truck. King had a house and a Jaguar? Really?

Once Sebastian got in the truck, I looked over at him. "How old is King?" I asked. Something else I realized I didn't know. It hadn't been important. I was so wrapped up in everything else that I didn't take the time to really get to know him. Past what I'd already known.

"Thirty-five," he replied.

"And you?" I asked.

He grinned. "Not that damn old," he drawled, then added, "Twenty-eight."

I'd known King was older than me, but I hadn't realized he was eleven years older. Not that it mattered. What else did I not know?

"Where's his house?"

Sebastian glanced at me, then back at the road. "About five miles from here. It's on Salazar property. His father's house is there, along with their stables."

More stables?

We were already at Maeme's, and Sebastian put the truck in park and turned back to me. "Any more questions before I take you inside?"

I realized I suddenly had several, but asking him instead of King felt like I was doing something wrong. These are things I should have asked King about. I bit my bottom lip to keep from blurting out another question and shook my head.

Sebastian chuckled. "You're full of questions, but I respect the fact that you're gonna wait and ask King the rest."

I reached for the door handle and opened it. If I was going to wait, I had to get out of the truck.

"You're handling the engagement well. I thought it would bother you more."

I paused then and replayed what he'd just said in my head.

Engagement? What engagement? Whose engagement?

"Fuck," he muttered under his breath when I finally glanced back at him.

The way his brows were drawn together didn't ease the slowly rising anxiety in my chest. Something wasn't okay. I just didn't want to reach out and grab the truth just yet.

"Look, I thought he'd told you. When he left Scotlin at his house and came here last night, I thought he was coming to tell you."

Scotlin had stayed at his house? The house I hadn't even known existed? A sick dread began to pool in my stomach.

"What … what do you mean?" I choked out as my hand tightened its grip on the door.

"It's just a job."

"What is just a job?" I demanded this time.

"The engagement. One of us had to do it, and King was the only one that made sense. With his and Scotlin's history, it was believable."

I just sat there, staring straight ahead. Out into the yard that was lit with little lights buried in the ground. Was I understanding him correctly? Was he telling me that King was engaged to Scotlin? For a job? What kind of job was that?

"I'm gonna be his damn punching bag for this," Sebastian muttered.

"I … I need to go inside," I managed to say and grabbed my bag before getting down out of the truck.

I had to get away from him, from everyone, and think this through. Take a moment. Revaluate everything I thought I had known. Again.

"Rumor," Sebastian called out. "Wait!"

I did not wait. I kept walking. I had to get to that door. Get to the blue room and close myself away.

"Rumor, please," he added.

I heard him jog up behind me.

I shook my head. "I got enough information for one night."

"I thought you knew. I'm sorry. This isn't something he wants to do. He has to. It's to keep her safe. There is shit going down, and she has a stalker. That's why he's having to stay the night at his house with her now."

I stopped and placed a hand on my stomach as I inhaled sharply. That hit harder than I'd been ready for. They were together. At his house. Where his bed was. All night. He was protecting her. I'd seen her, and I knew without being told that she liked him. She hadn't been able to keep her hands off him.

What about me? He didn't want to protect me anymore? He was choosing to be her protector now?

"I'm making this worse," he said.

"I, uh … good night," I replied and bolted for the door before he could say anything more to me.

· SIX ·

The night couldn't fix the reality of the next day.

RUMOR

Maeme met me at the door, and her face instantly tensed as she took a good look at me. When she let out a sigh and reached for my hand to pull me inside, I felt myself start to crumble. If she tried to make me talk about this right now, I was going to fall apart. I needed some time to process it all.

"King's gonna kill him," she said with a shake of her head. "I need to go run interference. Go on up to the blue room and take a nice, long bubble bath. Don't think about this."

If it were only that easy to put all I had learned from my mind. But I wanted to be alone, so I just nodded.

She gave my hand a squeeze, then let it go. "I'll bring you up something to eat soon."

There was no point. I had no appetite. "I'm not hungry," I told her, walking toward the stairs.

"Then, I'll bring wine."

I didn't turn that down. Perhaps enough of it would numb this pain.

I was almost to the bedroom door when I heard Maeme's voice demand, "What did you tell her?"

I didn't wait to listen to any more of the conversation and closed myself off inside. As I stared at the bed, my thoughts went to last night and all that I'd done with King on that bed. The sheets would smell like him. I closed my eyes and winced at the idea of having to sleep there.

He was in a fake engagement to a gorgeous blonde he had history with. They were at his house, which I hadn't even known about, and sleeping there. He was protecting her. Nothing about that could end well—at least for me. I had read this book before. Fake engagements, fake marriages, falling in love with the body-guard. They had been some of my favorite romance tropes, but now … I hated them. All of them. Every single one.

My eyes stung as I walked through the room, dropping my bag on the bed and then heading to the en suite. Slipping my hand into the pocket of my shorts, I pulled out the phone and laid it on the counter, then stared at myself in the mirror.

The insults Hill had thrown at me all came rushing back. My top lip was too big, my hair too untamed, my skin too dark, my bottom teeth weren't perfectly straight. I wasn't stunning, like the women I'd seen with King. Like the woman in his house with him now. I knew I wasn't ugly, but I had flaws. Enough that when put together, it made me very average.

Perhaps if I had a good sense of humor, then it would make up for where I was lacking, but my personality was lacking, at best. I'd had so many horrors in my past that I wasn't friendly. I didn't look on the bright side of things. I didn't even have a high school diploma. I had a GED. Turning eighteen and being kicked out of state care halfway through my senior year had caused me to have to drop out. So, I didn't even have a proper education and intelligence to fill in the gaps.

Scotlin was the kind of female that people expected King to be with. She was all the things I was not. She also knew him in ways that I didn't. He'd taken her to his house. They had grown up together.

Me, on the other hand? I didn't even know his favorite color.

There was a knock on my bedroom door before I heard it open.

"I have the wine," Maeme announced just before she appeared in the bathroom doorway.

She held up an open bottle of red wine with a stemmed glass in the other. I watched as she sat it down then filled the glass more than halfway before sliding it over to me.

"I'll go run your bath water. Drink."

I didn't argue. I took the glass and placed it to my lips. The cherry scent was one I was familiar with. Pinot noir had been Hill's favorite wine.

"I know Sebastian dropped the Scotlin stuff on you, just like I know what you were doing in here last night with King," she said as she bent over the tub, feeling the water temperature. "I'm sorry you found out the way you did. I'm not blind, and I can tell you've got feelings for King. This all must be real confusing for you. You've taken in a lot of information the past two weeks."

She poured some pearly-colored liquid into the running water, then sprinkled in some bath salts before straightening and turning back to me.

"I don't like you being hurt and upset. You've had enough of that in your short life. So, I am telling you now that I love my grandson, but he ain't the kind of man you need. You need the steady kind, the patient and romantic type of man. One who can erase all the ugly you've survived and give you nothing but good."

She walked over to me and wrapped her fingers around my arm gently. "The men in this family, they aren't that. They can't be. I was married to one. I raised two. It's not a life meant for all of us. My Gabriel loved me just as fiercely as I loved him, but that doesn't mean it wasn't a hard marriage. We went through a lot. I wasn't always happy. I've had to accept some hard things. And you ..." She paused, then reached up to pat my cheek. "You've had all the dark you need to in this life. You need to find the happy. The light.

The picket fence, children, husband who adores you. That's what you deserve. Not more darkness."

I managed a nod. I didn't say anything because I was afraid I'd let out a sob. Hearing her tell me this and realizing I'd been so wrapped up in King and how I felt with him that I hadn't thought of the big picture. The one where he wasn't interested in marriage and family. He enjoyed beating women who wanted it. He'd loved the little spanking he gave me.

And not once had he even hinted that this was a long-term thing. There were no proclamations of love from him. He hadn't lied about that. He'd made it clear that it was the sex he wanted from me. Never had he tried to bring me into his life more.

The small things I should have known about him that I didn't were made very apparent tonight.

"I'm going to leave you with that bottle of my favorite wine and let you soak in the bath. Get some sleep. Tomorrow, things will be brighter. They always are."

I didn't believe that because I knew for a fact that it wasn't true. The night couldn't fix the reality of the next day.

"Good night," I told her.

"Good night, Rumor," she replied, then left me there.

I watched the water fill the tub as I drank from the glass in my hand.

Before King, I had sworn off men. I said I would never put myself in a situation for another one to hurt me. Yet I had fallen so easily. It had taken very little effort on his part.

No more. I was going to cry tonight, drink this wine, feel sorry for myself, but in the morning, I was done. With all men. I just needed me in this world. Relying on others was foolish. Even if they were as kind as Maeme. I had to learn to take care of me. No leaning on someone else.

My phone buzzed, and I froze, not wanting to look down at it. I was planning my survival steps. Reading a text from King was not going to help me. Without looking at the screen, I turned off the phone and went and put it away in the closet. Out of sight. I didn't need the temptation to turn it on and read what he had said. Whatever it was, it didn't matter.

The wine had helped me sleep. That was the one thing I could think of to be thankful for this morning. I hadn't tossed and turned all night. Once I washed my face, brushed my teeth, and got dressed, I did feel somewhat better. Sure, if I allowed myself to dwell on things, I might burst into tears, but I was fighting it with all I had.

Focus on the positive. I hadn't woken up married to Hill. I wasn't going to be beaten today. No more cracked ribs and busted lips. There were books waiting on me to read. I could eat whatever I wanted for breakfast. I didn't have to step on a scale this morning to have my weight checked.

That pep talk seemed to push back the ache enough for me to leave the bedroom and go face Maeme. I had thought about all she'd said while I soaked last night. The more I drank while in the hot water, the more my thoughts got foggy. The numbing started to take effect. That was when I had gotten out and gone directly to bed.

I could smell breakfast before I even got to the bottom step. I listened for voices as I made my way in that direction. I heard no one, and the relief that came from that was instant. I didn't want to face King today or tomorrow. Perhaps a week maybe. A month. Would that be enough time?

What if he fell in love with Scotlin? What if this fake engagement and forced proximity caused him to develop feelings? I stopped walking and pressed my hand against my chest to ease the sharp pain that struck me at the thought. If that happened, how would I survive it?

"Rumor? Is that you?" Maeme called out.

I stared back at the kitchen doorway. I had to reply. Go in there. Not look like I was going to be sick. I was letting my imagination get away with me. I had to calm down and find a way not to care.

Maeme stepped into the hallway. "There you are," she said with a bright smile. "I thought I'd heard you. Come on in and eat."

I followed her into the kitchen. No one was here. There was something positive I could add to my list.

"You need to get out. See something other than this place and the Shephards. We are going to Annette's for afternoon tea. Her stylist is coming, and we are going to do some shopping. You need some things that are your own, and there is nothing Annette loves more than to host a fashion show in her sitting room."

I was leaving the property? Going to Storm's parents' home?

"Is that safe?" I asked her, not sure if I should be going anywhere, as lovely as the idea sounded.

Maeme handed me a plate. "Yes. Storm is taking us, and the Kingston property is as secure as we are here."

King wasn't taking us. He wasn't here to talk to me either. No explanation or even an apology. I was relieved he wasn't here, but then it also stung. I'd wanted him to care enough that he'd at least try and talk to me.

Not wanting Maeme to see that I was upset, I focused on getting food on my plate, then took a seat at the bar.

She set a cup of coffee down in front of me. "It has Splenda and almond milk in it," she told me.

I looked up at her. "Thank you," I replied, surprised that she had both of those things.

"King told me you prefer almond milk in your coffee instead of creamer."

King had told her. That was thoughtful. NO! I wasn't going there. King was manipulative. He had kept things from me. He had probably had sex with Scotlin last night.

My grip on the fork in my hand tightened, and I took in a slow, deep breath. I had to stop thinking about him.

· SEVEN ·

I'd missed so many red flags in my desire to belong to someone.

RUMOR

Barrett and Annette Kingston's home wasn't as stupendous as the Shephards', but it had the historical architecture that made it breathtaking. Two hundred years ago, this would have been considered a mansion.

Maeme sat up front with Storm in the black Escalade he had arrived to pick us up in.

I'd listened to their conversation and responded when Maeme brought me into it, but for the most part, I had taken in the landscape as we drove. It had been dark when I arrived here over a month ago now.

The town was beautiful. Like something out of a history book. The homes that we'd passed were antebellum, and many had historical markers. I was so caught up in it all that I missed when Maeme spoke to me more than once. She chuckled at my distraction and informed me that Madison was Georgia's best small town, according to the internet. But she believed it was the best town in the South. She also told me that it had been named for President James Madison.

I understood why they had all chosen to live here and not leave. Who would want to leave?

Storm opened the car door for me, and as I stepped out, I saw one of the large double doors to the front of the house swing open. Annette came outside, dressed in a pencil-straight white skirt that hit just above the knee and a sleeveless dark blue button-up blouse that was tucked in at the waist. She was always so well groomed and dressed. I wondered if she ever had a hair out of place.

"I expect mint juleps are on the veranda," Maeme called out to her.

Annette laughed. "They're already made and waiting on us."

"You grew up in this house?" I asked Storm.

He nodded. "Yep. Third generation of Kingstons to live in it."

Wow. What it must be like to have that kind of family history. To know who you had come from, where they'd lived, what their names were. Things I would never know about myself.

"It's beautiful," I told him.

"The azaleas are coming in nicely," Maeme called out to Annette as she walked over to me.

"Aren't they?! I love spring," she replied. "Wait until you see my tulips out back. They are to die for."

Maeme stopped a few feet from me and waved a hand for me to come with her.

"Good luck," Storm whispered as I left him there.

Getting a change of scenery was helping my mood. The ache in my chest was still there, but it was easier to push it back and think about other things this way. I walked beside Maeme up to the front steps that led onto the porch.

Annette opened her door and motioned for us to go inside. "Come on in. Our drinks await," she informed us.

This kind of thing was what made it hard to associate these people with what I knew of the Mafia. They seemed wholesome and normal.

You would never imagine that Maeme could shoot a pistol, much less that she owned one. I wondered if Annette had a gun.

Could she shoot one too? Was that part of the prerequisite to marrying one of these men?

"You look perfect in that pink sundress," Annette told me. "I bought that for Lela, and she never wore it. I'm so happy you are getting some use out of the things I sent." Her gaze dropped to my sandals. "We will definitely do some shoe shopping today."

"Annette," Maeme scolded.

Her eyes swung up to meet Maeme's. "I wasn't saying anything was wrong with the ones she is wearing. I like Tory Burch. It's just that she seems to always be wearing them. She needs more shoes."

Maeme rolled her eyes and looked at me. "You'll end up with more shoes than you know what to do with today."

I started to argue that I didn't need more, but the hopeful expression on Annette's face stopped me. Instead, I managed a smile. "As long as the cost comes out of Hill's—uh, my money." It was hard to think of it as mine.

Nothing that had been Hill's ever felt like mine. Even before we married, he made it clear that he owned everything. I'd missed so many red flags in my desire to belong to someone. To have a family.

Once, I had daydreamed about having kids of my own. Being the mom I'd never had. Knowing that there was someone who was a part of me. That I shared their blood. But now, I didn't see that in my future. It was a dream I had let go of after the first broken rib. I'd realized then that I couldn't bring a child into that life. Hill was dead, but my trust in men was once again gone.

The inside of the Kingstons' home made me feel as if I had stepped into the pages of *Gone with the Wind*. The furnishings, although in mint condition, were all from the era in which this house was built. I could just see Scarlett O'Hara descending the open, sweeping stairway that greeted us in the enormous foyer.

"Your home is stunning," I told her as I took in the chandelier and ornate touches to not only the furniture, but also the architecture itself.

"Thank you. It is a labor of love. There always seems to be something that needs fixing or updating. Barrett's grandfather originally bought this house. Over the decades, the furnishings have been restored and updated some, but we like to keep it as true to character as we can."

"Speaking of which, have you gotten the floor refinished in the ballroom?" Maeme asked.

The nervous glance that Annette flashed at me before quickly turning her gaze to Maeme was odd. Why had that questioned bothered her? It seemed innocent enough.

"Yes. Those are complete. I can show you later," she replied with a fake smile where her real one used to be.

"She knows about the engagement, Annette. It's okay," Maeme told her, then looked at me. "The engagement party is going to be held here."

My stomach knotted up. They were having an engagement party. That made it feel very real. How far were they planning on going with the fake relationship?

"Oh, thank goodness," Annette breathed. "I was so worried I'd slip up and say something. Storm seemed to think it was very important that I not mention it around Rumor." Her eyes shone with sympathy as she glanced back at me.

"Can I use your bathroom?" I blurted, needing a moment to get myself pulled back together after this news sent me back to the dark hole I'd been trying to climb out of.

"Of course," Annette said, flicking her gaze to Maeme with clear concern in her expression. "Right this way."

I followed her as I mentally began checking off my list of things to be thankful for. Again.

There was no more mention of the engagement party, the ballroom, or King. All the talk was about the flowers, what had bloomed, what was going to bloom, Lela's decision to get her master's degree, and the Kentucky Derby next weekend.

When Storm arrived to take us back to Maeme's, I had eight new pairs of shoes, five dresses, seven new everyday outfits, and two formal dresses that were breathtaking, but I had no idea why I would ever need one. I found arguing with Annette over clothing was pointless. She ignored me and had things packed up for me whether I thought I needed them or not.

Storm only grinned with amusement when his mom pointed out the bags and boxes of items she'd said I must have and told him to load them in the car.

· EIGHT ·

*This world I live in isn't one that builds strong relationships.
It rips them apart.*

RUMOR

I wanted the security and solitude of the little white cottage, but I understood that it was for my safety that Maeme had Storm bring me and all my new things inside her house. I felt bad that she wouldn't let me help him carry it all inside. When she was done telling him where to take everything and walked off, I turned to him.

"I'm sorry about all this stuff," I whispered. I couldn't go anywhere, so all the clothing seemed pointless.

"I have two sisters, and you just spent quality time with my mom. No need to apologize," he assured me, then winked as he turned and headed back out the door for more of my things.

I stood there, unsure what to do with myself when I heard a car door slam and voices outside. Walking over to the still-open front door, I looked out to see King's truck. My heart did a flutter, then remembered his fake engagement, and sank.

"Stay out of it!" King shouted as he came stalking up the walkway.

What had Storm said to him?

I backed up and thought about running to the blue room, but I wasn't sure I'd have time. Instead, I headed to the library. I could hide in there. I didn't want to see him or talk to him. Not yet.

There was a soft click as I closed the door and backed up farther into the room. I'd left the lights off in hopes he would see the room was dark and pass on by it.

"Where is she, Maeme?" I heard King demand.

"I know you're not coming in my house, yelling like a hothead."

"Maeme, I love you, but if you don't tell me where she is right this minute, I'm going to start breaking shit."

"Jesus, King!" Storm said. "Stop with the yelling."

"Where is she?" King said with a growl that startled me.

"You take one more step inside this house, and I WILL be the one breaking shit." Maeme's voice had taken on an edge I'd never heard before. She was angry … really angry.

"I need to talk to her." King's dark tone had softened somewhat.

"Not like this. She knows about your engagement. I reckon she needs some time to process all this," Maeme told him.

"FAKE! It's a fake engagement. Maeme, I've been forced to follow around a woman I don't particularly like. I'm being kept from talking to the woman I do want to be around, and I am real fucking close to snapping. SOMEONE is going to tell me where she is. Now!"

Unable to let this go on any longer, I decided I had better face him before this escalated any further. I hurried back out of the library and into the foyer while King was now yelling at Storm.

"Stop it!" I said loud enough to be heard over the noise.

King spun around, his eyes locking on me.

"Rumor."

He said my name with such relief that I felt guilty. I had no reason to feel such an emotion, but the mental abuse I'd suffered from my marriage warped me. My immediate reaction seemed to be to blame myself for whatever was wrong.

"I'll talk to you if you stop yelling at everyone," I replied.

He started walking in my direction, and Maeme stepped in front of him with her hands on her small hips. "She said she'd talk to you, not that you could invade her personal space."

King's nostrils flared as he looked down at his tiny grandmother.

"It's fine, Maeme. Really. We can go talk in the library," I said.

She glanced back at me, then sighed. "Very well. But this"—she turned back to King—"this'd better not blow up in our faces. You have a job to do."

King's eyes swung back up to meet mine, and he stepped around Maeme, then started toward me again. I didn't want to stand there and let him reach me. I preferred we talk about whatever it was he was intent on saying in private. Going back to the library, I mentally coached myself on how to handle this. I wasn't sure what to expect from him. But whatever it was, I would deal with it. I had to.

The door closed with more force than necessary behind me, and I spun around to see King looking at me as if I were his last meal before he closed the distance between us.

"Your phone is off and has been since last night. I've tried calling and texting all fucking night and day," he said as he grabbed my chin, tilting my head back. "It's not a real engagement. They told you that. It's fake. So, what is wrong?"

"You have a house," I blurted. Not the smoothest response, but it must have been what was bothering me the most.

He nodded. "Yeah. So?"

I grabbed his arm and pulled his hand from my face. "So, I didn't know. You're keeping a woman there, at a house I didn't know you had. I've never seen it." I paused and crossed my arms over my chest. "We've had sex. A lot. But I don't know things about you. Things like that. It … it just made it clear that all we are doing is physical, and I don't think I can do that."

His eyes narrowed as he studied me, trying to make sense of my words.

"You're upset because you didn't know I had a house?"

I nodded. "Yes. I don't know your favorite color … or … or your favorite flavor ice cream or what you like to do … your hobbies."

The corner of his mouth twitched as he held my gaze, making me feel slightly ridiculous. Saying this all out loud made it seem silly. I wasn't verbalizing this well.

"Green—the color of your eyes, to be exact. Peanut butter cup ice cream—the kind with the actual chunks in it. When I was younger, I played football. Quarterback. I could have played in college, but I didn't get that option in the family. I had to grow up. Take my place in the ranks. But I still love to throw a ball. I like watching it too," he said, reaching out to run a knuckle over my cheek. "Being with you. That's become my favorite thing to do in my free time."

Was he aware the power he wielded with his eyes alone? Probably. He was a grown man. He had been reeling in women since I had been in preschool. Yet here I was, feeling that pull. The desire to agree to whatever he wanted if I could have him.

"You're thirty-five," I said, not sure as to why I needed to point that out.

He grinned then. "Yeah, sweets, I am." He cupped the side of my face. "You decided I'm too old for you?"

I rolled my eyes, and he chuckled, stepping closer to me. The heat from his body made me tremble, and I really wished it hadn't. I wished I could stop this and walk away. Save myself from being hurt. Because I knew I would be. I'd already suffered some of the pain that would come from loving this man.

"What else do you want to know?" he asked, lowering his head to nuzzle near my ear.

My eyes began to flutter closed, and I had to use all the strength I could muster to step back from him. His hand fell away, but he didn't take his eyes off me.

"Are you sleeping with her?" I asked before I could stop myself. It was an answer I knew could break me, but I had to know.

His brows drew together. "Scotlin?"

"Yes," I said through clenched teeth.

Who else would I be asking about? Was there someone else I needed to be asking about?

"Fuck no." The disgusted look on his face was like a balm to my soul.

"Why? She's beautiful. She likes you. She's living in your house."

He took a step in my direction, and I backed up, keeping the space between us.

The hurt in his gaze made it hard for me to stand firm. A large part of me wanted to run to him, wrap my arms around him, and beg him to just want me. It was pathetic.

He let out a deep sigh. "Yes, Scotlin is a beautiful woman. She chased after me for years, but she was four years younger than I was, and I ignored it. Until she turned nineteen and began pursuing me hard. Showing up everywhere that I was." He shook his head. "I eventually gave in, and we had a relationship of sorts."

This wasn't helping me. In fact, this was much worse than I had anticipated. He'd had a relationship with her. It wasn't a fling, like I had assumed. I wished I had sat down before he started telling me their past.

"She got pregnant. I told her I'd marry her. But she didn't want to be a mom. Ever. So, without talking to me about it, she went and had an abortion."

My hand went to my stomach as I let out a gasp. "Oh, King," I breathed. I'd not expected that.

His blue eyes locked on me. "And that was the end of us. I didn't want to marry her. It would have been a horrible mistake. I know that now, but at the time, I just wanted to do the right thing. Give my kid what I hadn't had—parents who were together. I even convinced myself I could love her if I tried." A hard laugh fell from his lips.

"So, no, I'm not fucking Scotlin. I will never fuck Scotlin again. Over the years, we made peace with the past. Our families are connected. I can't call her a friend because I don't trust her. I don't even like being around her. But this is a job I have to see through. Even if I hate every fucking moment."

When he took a step toward me, this time, I didn't move.

"I'm so sorry," I breathed as I stared up at him.

"Long time ago, sweets," he said, running his hands up my bare arms. "Now, tell me, what else do you want to know? Ask anything. I'll tell you."

What else did I want to know? He'd hit me with this information that made my chest ache for him. I couldn't ask him to share anything else. What other skeletons were in his closet that I could unintentionally drag out? I didn't think I was ready for that.

"That's enough," I replied.

"That's all you need to know? You sure? Because I *do not* want to go through another day like that again. I hate being away from you and not being able to check in on you. It fucks with my head, sweets."

I did have another question. One I had to ask. If what he was doing, what we were doing, wasn't going away. If he was going to keep talking to me like this. Making me feel these things. I had to ask.

"What are we? You … you say we're friends, but this … this doesn't feel like friends, King. This feels like more, and to me, it is more. And if it's not more to you, then I can't keep doing it and survive it. Survive you."

"You're right. We're not friends. I thought we could be, but I need you. I want you with me all the damn time. When shit gets dark, all it takes is your smile to ease the demons inside. Does it need a label?"

Yes. No. Ugh! Why was I pushing? This was all new. Perhaps I was too inexperienced in life and I was asking for something I shouldn't.

"I guess not," I replied.

His hands grabbed my waist and pulled me against him. "Those eyes of yours are saying something different. You want security. Your trust in me is gone, and I deserve it." He lowered his head and pressed a kiss to the corner of my mouth. "I don't know what to call this. I just know you're all I think about. The only one I want to fuck. The only person I miss. Yeah, it sounds like a relationship, but I've seen what happens when people fall in love. That shit isn't real. It's just a word. It ends in disaster, and I could never live with myself if that happened to us and I lost you. My life … this world I live in isn't one that builds strong relationships. It rips them apart. I've seen it happen over and over. So, let's not label it. Let's just live in the moment. Enjoy how this feels."

There were no right words here. At least, I couldn't think of any. I just nodded, and he brushed his lips against mine as his hands tightened their hold on me.

"When this is over, move into my house with me," he said, then nipped at my top lip with his teeth.

"What?" I asked, breathless.

"You heard me."

"When what is over?" I asked him, needing clarification as my heart soared.

He trailed kisses over to my ear and pressed a kiss to the tender spot beneath it. I shivered, and my hands fisted in his shirt.

"When I find Scotlin's stalker and the Insantos are handled, I want you in my house. With me."

The way the heaviness from earlier lifted from my shoulders should have been a warning. One for me. Reminding me just how much power he had over me. Every step I took closer to him, I was only losing more of my heart. And he didn't believe in relationships.

King wrapped his larger hand around mine and flashed me a crooked grin as he led me out the door of the library. He didn't slow his pace as we reached the foyer, where Maeme and Storm still stood.

"She's going with me for the rest of the day," King informed them without pausing for a response.

"What about tonight?" Maeme asked him. "You're Scotlin's date at her father's dinner party this evening."

I would not let that bother me. I had to find a way to control the jealous surge that came whenever I heard her name and that King would be with her. If I was going to do this with him, I had to trust him even if he'd done little to earn my trust back.

King's grip on my hand tightened. "Rumor can stay in my room at the stables while I go. I'll come back there tonight when it is over."

"What about Scotlin?" Storm asked, causing King to tense up.

"She'll be staying at her father's," he said through clenched teeth.

"Rumor, is this what you want?" Maeme asked.

I shifted my gaze from King to his grandmother. The concern in her expression was clear. She didn't think I should go, but how did I explain to her that I wanted to be with him, even after everything that had happened?

"Yes," I replied.

She let out a long sigh, then nodded. "Very well."

King pulled me with him out the door before either of them could say more. I had to almost run to keep up with his pace all the way to the truck.

"You didn't ask me about this," I said to him as we stopped at the passenger door. "What if I didn't want to go with you?"

His eyes snapped to mine. "You don't want to go with me?"

That wasn't the point.

"I don't even have my things."

King moved in front of me, caging me against the side of his truck. "Sweets, I fucked up. But you've forgiven me. I know you drew your lines, and there were rules, but after the other night and that conversation we just had in the library, I assumed things had changed. You might not trust me, but you don't want me with another woman. I don't want another woman. So, we agree on that. Now, I want to fuck you. I want you in my room, in my bed, in my shower. The best I can do right now is take you to my room in the stables. Keeping you there. With my things. You're safe there. It's safer than even Maeme's. I won't have to worry when I can't be with you. Please." He paused and wrapped an arm around my waist, holding me against his body. "Don't fight me on this. The two weeks I went without being inside your hot little cunt were fucking brutal."

I swallowed hard and felt my body melt against his as I leaned in closer without even realizing I was doing it. "Okay." My voice was barely above a whisper.

"That's my girl," he replied with a slow grin spreading across his face. "Let's go before I fuck you against this damn truck and Maeme puts a bullet in my ass."

He reached behind me to open the door while pulling me away from the truck and with him as he stepped back.

• NINE •

Did that make me deranged?

RUMOR

Sleeping on sheets that smelled like King was nothing compared to walking back into his room at the stables. Being away from it, I had forgotten how his scent clung to the space. Would his house be like this too? Everywhere I went, I'd be engulfed in King. As if he needed anything more to make me weak and stupid.

"How did you acquire a room here? Since you have a house?" I asked as he dropped his keys on the dresser.

He smirked. "Once, Wilder, Thatcher, and I all stayed out here. Wilder moved out first. He got a girl pregnant, and they married. Our twenties were fun here, but the closer we got to thirty, we wanted something of our own. Thatcher had a house built farther back on this property. I did the same on the Salazar land, but I kept my room here. Comes in handy when I need to be close."

He walked to me and loomed over me, his gaze trailing along my features as he did so. "I hadn't stayed here in months, but once I got you settled in the shotgun house, I wanted to be close. Make sure I was here if you needed anything. I moved back in. Until last night, I hadn't slept at my house since your second night here."

That was something. He'd stayed close for me. He might not admit it or put a name to it, but he had felt something from day one. Even if I had been a nervous mess, I could admit I'd found him attractive.

He moved quickly then, taking me by surprise, and scooped me up in his arms.

"King!" I squealed, wrapping my arms around his neck as he walked me over to the sofa and sank down on it with me in his lap.

"Ask," he said, keeping his arms around my waist.

"Ask what?"

The charming grin that should come with a warning label touched his lips. "Everything. What do you want to know?"

Unsure why he was doing this, I tried to read his expression. "Why?" I finally asked.

His hand moved up my back and tugged on my hair playfully. "Because you want to know, and when I strip you naked and fuck you in the shower, I'd like all your thoughts to be on that. Us. So, ask me, sweets. What is going on in that head of yours?"

A nervous laugh tumbled from my lips as I dropped my gaze down to study the front of his shirt. "No pressure or anything," I replied.

He pulled back on my hair hard enough to tilt my head back until my eyes met his.

"It's not a test. I'm simply telling you that you can ask me whatever you want. I'll answer. Even if I don't want to."

I was torn. Afraid of the things I might not want to know. But aware I needed to know before I went any further. Loving a man who didn't see a future in any relationship was brave. It would be the bravest thing I'd done. Running from Hill had been reckless and desperate. I couldn't think of it as brave. But this ... this I had time to consider. He would leave me one day. This would end, and right now, this emotion, which was so much stronger than anything I had ever experienced, I knew it was love. The reclusive thing I had always sought and never truly found. I knew the real thing now. At least how it felt for me.

Perhaps that was all I was meant to experience. Love was a gift that wasn't promised to anyone. Right now, King wanted me, and I knew without question that I was going to do this. Take whatever he gave me.

"When is your birthday?" I asked him.

"July 27," he replied. "And yours is May 21."

I leaned back, surprised that he knew that.

"Sweets, Mafia. Remember? We knew everything about Churchill Millroe before we broke into his house that day. Including the security system code, his schedule, his wife's schedule," he replied, wrapping my hair around his fist. "Rumor Ariella LeBlanc."

Hearing my name—the one on my birth certificate—caused me to still. If he knew that, how long had he known? Since the moment he'd picked me up at the service station?

"Sweets," he said in a gentle tone, letting go of my hair to touch my cheek, "the Mafia, baby, we don't leave anything unturned. We are thorough. The bastard changed your name, but that didn't erase it."

I'd begged Hill to let me keep the name Ariella. I wasn't one hundred percent positive, but I'd been told that my mother's name was Ariella. She'd named me after herself. It could have been a lie, but I clung to it. Wanted it to be true because it had given me a beginning. Someone I had belonged to. Had a connection to. When Hill had taken it from me, completely wiping out the only history I had, I'd mourned it.

"I want it back," I said.

He nodded. "Okay. We'll change it back."

I stared at him. "I can do that?"

King leaned in close, pressing a kiss to my chin. "Yeah, sweets, we can."

The swell of joy inside my chest, spreading through me, was one of those rare things.

Leaning back to look at me, King narrowed his eyes slightly as he studied me. "Those unshed tears are happy, right?" he asked.

I nodded my head and ran my hands up his arms to grab his biceps, and they flexed under my touch. "What was that about a shower?"

He flashed a wicked grin at me. "You're done with the questions? You didn't ask my full name."

I leaned closer to him. "King Chasen Salazar."

His eyes widened.

"Maeme called you that the first night you brought me here," I reminded him.

"And you remembered? With all the shit you'd dealt with that day?" He seemed surprised.

I lifted a shoulder. "I was terrified, running from the cops, but I was still a female who had been rescued by the most beautiful man she'd ever met."

King gripped my waist and lifted me off him, standing me up. "Beautiful? Really? Not sexy? Charming?" he asked as he stood.

"Those things too," I replied.

A deep, pleased sound came from his chest as he reached for my sundress and tugged it up, sliding it over my hips until it was bunched at my waist.

"Lift your hands."

I did as told and let him take it the rest of the way off me. Standing there in nothing but a pair of white satin panties, I stared up at him. His appreciative gaze drifted down my body as he ran a hand down my back until he was cupping my butt. When he squeezed it, a low groan came from him.

"Let me spank it."

Tingles danced throughout my body. I didn't try to speak, giving him a nod. The flare of heat in his blue depths caused me to shiver. He enjoyed this. And as terrified as it seemed I should be, I knew what he wanted to do was nothing like what I'd experienced with Hill.

King brought pleasure with each strike. His words were seductive, addictive, not painful and degrading. I couldn't imagine ever trusting anyone else like this, but with him, it was easy. I wanted it too. His arousal only spurred mine on.

He sat back down, then took my hand in his and pulled me over his lap. I gasped and tensed, turning to stare up at him. This wasn't what I'd been expecting. His focus wasn't on me though. He seemed transfixed on my bottom as he ran his hand over it, slipping his fingertips just underneath the edge of my panties.

"Relax," he murmured.

That seemed like an impossible task in this position. The uncertainty, mixed with the helplessness and sense of being exposed, was exciting. Did that make me deranged?

His hand lifted slowly before coming down with a firm, hard smack, causing me to jump. A rumble of pleasure came from him as he brushed his fingertips over the skin that was currently stinging.

"So damn pretty," he said before lifting his hand.

I closed my eyes and turned away from him with the impact. The sharp pang was followed by an ache of pleasure between my legs. King did it again and again. Each time, it was harder, and I could hear his breathing getting heavier. The hard ridge of his erection pressed against my belly, only building the thrill into a frenzy.

"Fuck, sweets. I love seeing your ass red," he said in a husky tone as he grabbed a cheek and squeezed the tender flesh. "Such a good girl." His hand caressed the skin that currently stung. "Goddamn, this ass is juicy."

I trembled from the dark edge in his voice.

"Get up!" he ordered.

I moved quickly. Unsure of what was happening, but the sudden fear was tinted with the thrill.

"Hands on the bed. Ass in the air," he demanded, standing and shoving me toward it.

I stumbled, confused by the sudden change in him. The gleam in his eye wasn't something I'd seen before. I was torn between wanting to run or doing as he'd said. His hand slapped against my already-tender bottom with enough force to cause me to fall forward, catching myself on the edge of the bed.

My heart slammed against my chest wildly. What had happened to him? Why was he doing this? I grabbed fistfuls of the quilt and closed my eyes tightly. With one hard jerk, King pulled my panties down to my ankles, then tugged them free before pushing my legs open wider.

The sound of him inhaling deeply came just before the hot, possessive lick of his tongue slid between my legs. A cry tore from me as my knees buckled.

"I'm gonna eat this sweet pussy until you squirt on my face," he said as he lapped at me, making my world spin. "Soaking wet from me spanking that ass."

He growled then and slipped a finger inside me. "Twists me up, sweets."

I let out a cry and pressed back, wanting to feel more. "Please," I begged.

"Please what? What is it you need?"

I clawed at the bed as my body shook. "You. I need you. Inside me."

The hard crack of his hand on my butt pulled a strangled moan from me. Then, he did it again. And again.

"I said I wanted you to squirt on my face," he said. "Don't distract me."

I opened my mouth to beg or apologize. I wasn't sure, but King's tongue sliding up between my butt cheeks cut off all words. My eyes flew open in shock. He flicked at the hole, and I tightened. The sheer exposure of this was too much.

"Easy," he whispered against my untouched area. "Just let me play a little."

I stared at the wall, holding my breath as he pulled my cheeks open, pressed his face there, and then made a pleased hum as his tongue tickled the opening again.

"Oh God!" I moaned, burying my face in the mattress, not believing he was doing this.

"That's a good girl," he praised as he began to trail kisses along my bottom.

He shoved two fingers between my legs this time, and I immediately rocked back, desperate for it. My body was spiraling in areas I hadn't known it could feel things.

This time, when I felt the tip of his tongue skim the outer rim, then trail down to meet where his fingers were thrusting inside of me, the bliss that had been creeping closer burst free. The warm rush that came between my legs shook me as I held on to the covers while wave after wave of my climax came over me.

King's hands grabbed my waist, and for a brief moment, I felt airborne before my back hit the bed and his massive body came over me. The wild look in his eyes made me whimper with another jolt between my legs.

"Fuck, baby girl. You make me crazy," he swore before grabbing my knees and holding my legs open wide as he slammed inside of me.

"AH!" tore from my lips as he held nothing back.

With a ferocity I'd never experienced, King began to fuck me. Each punch of his hips against mine got more aggressive.

"Tell me whose pussy this is," he demanded.

My eyes locked on his. The blue almost completely taken over by his pupils.

"Yours," I said, hoping that was what he wanted to hear me say.

"Fuuuck," he groaned loudly.

I watched him, completely mesmerized by him. I was sure I'd never see anything that could compare to the beauty of King Salazar in this moment. His body jerked, and his jaw slackened slightly just before I felt the pulse inside of me.

The image he'd created, along with the sensation of his release filling me, ignited, sending me into yet another realm of bliss.

· T E N ·

I'd think with all that crying out and moaning I heard,
you'd be in a better mood.

KING

Storm stepped out of Sword's stall just as I was about to pass,
headed for the exit.

"Wearing a tux, huh? Sounds like a good time," he said as he
locked the stallion inside.

"Hell is a more accurate description," I grumbled.

Leaving Rumor curled up in my bed, asleep, wasn't helping
my mood either. She had been exhausted after three rounds of
fucking. Once I'd taken her against the wall of the shower, I had
washed her hair and conditioned it, following her directions,
then bathed her body. She was so spent that she didn't even get
dressed. While I washed my hair, I watched her walk into the
bedroom and drop the towel, then climb under the covers. I'd cut
off my left hand if I could forget this shit tonight and go back up
there with her.

"I'd think with all that crying out and moaning I heard, you'd be
in a better mood. How many times did you two fuck? Or was it a
marathon round? Because if it was, then you need to tell me what
kind of pills you're taking to go that long."

My hands fisted at my sides as a monster seemed to stretch out inside my chest. I didn't like that he'd heard her. Not one fucking bit. Those sounds had been for me.

"Jesus," he muttered. "Get the murderous look off your face. It was loud. The guys outside probably heard it."

I didn't need this right now. I had to go deal with Scotlin all evening. Touching me. Pretending like I wanted to touch her. Fucking hell.

I stalked past Storm without saying anything. Just as I got to the door, I stopped and turned back to him.

"No one touches her. No one bothers her. No one gets close enough to breathe her air."

Storm held up both his hands. "Dude, she's safe."

I trusted him. Not that I had a lot of choice. If I wanted her here with me at nights and I wanted the peace of mind that she was safe, I had to trust them all.

Stepping outside, I did a quick scan of the area. Two of the trainers were out on our younger thoroughbreds. Stellan was with the jockey we were using for one of the Derby races and Bloodline, our hopeful for the Preakness Stakes. The area was secure, but then I hadn't expected any less. This place was locked down like a fortress.

A low whistle came from behind me as I made my way to the truck. I turned to see Thatcher leaning against the side of the barn with a cigarette between his teeth and his arms crossed over his chest.

"Hot date?" he asked with amusement in his grin.

"Fuck off," I replied.

He knew where I was going, just like he knew this was the last thing I wanted to do.

His twisted laugh didn't help my mood as I jerked my door open and climbing inside.

· E L E V E N ·

I decided that remaining silent was best.

RUMOR

Waking up with a note by the pillow from King, telling me he'd be back tonight, had put me in a funk. I'd known he had to go to dinner with Scotlin, but it didn't mean I liked it. Reminding myself it was me he had been with all afternoon helped ease the sadness some. The jealousy though was more difficult to tame.

Staying in the bedroom all evening wasn't going to help me either. I would just smell him and think about what he was doing. If she was touching him. If he was touching her. I had to get out of here and find a distraction.

I made my way downstairs and followed the sound of voices to the lounge room. The door was standing open as I looked inside. Sebastian was seated on one of the sofas with a piece of pizza in his hand and his focus on the large screen that covered the wall. I scanned the rest of the area to see Storm pouring a drink at the bar. Wells was seated in a leather chair when I found him. His attention was already on me.

He smiled at me. A slow, slightly devilish grin. "Come on in. Have some pizza."

I felt the other two sets of eyes in the room swing my way, and I stepped inside, shifting my gaze from Storm to Sebastian.

"You're awake," Storm said. "Pizza is on the table. Go get you some. I'll fix you a drink. What's your poison?"

The smell of the pizza hit me, and my stomach grumbled. I hadn't realized how hungry I was until now.

"Uh, water is fine," I replied.

"Water it is," he agreed.

"Come on. It's pizza. If you're not gonna have a beer, at least have a cocktail. We can make girlie shit," Wells said, opening the box of pizza on the table that sat in front of the main sofa.

"Water is fine. Really."

"Let her drink what the fuck she wants," Sebastian snapped at him.

Wells rolled his eyes and grabbed another slice of pizza, then sat back down.

I decided to take the seat on the same sofa as Sebastian. Wells made me uneasy. I had been around him the least of the guys. Granted, he didn't make me feel as edgy as Thatcher did though. Thankfully, he wasn't here.

"Aren't you leaving?" Sebastian asked, his gaze flickering over to Wells.

Wells finished chewing the food in his mouth and swallowed. "Yeah. Sure you two don't want to join me?"

Storm held out my glass of water to me, then glanced over at Wells. "I might later."

Wells smirked. "You got a thing for the new blonde, don't you?"

He shrugged. "I wouldn't call it a thing."

"When Storm gets a thing for someone, it'll be a cold day in hell," Sebastian said, leaning forward to take the box of pizza and slide it closer to me. "Don't be shy. Eat up."

Setting down my glass of water, I took a piece of pizza and placed it on a napkin.

"You've forgiven King," Wells said.

I glanced up at him. Had I forgiven King, or was it just unavoid-able? My need for him was stronger than the damage he'd done. I wasn't going to explain all that to Wells—or anyone for that mat-ter—so I just nodded, then took a bite of the pizza.

Wells chuckled as he stood up. "Looks like things are gonna get interesting then."

"Shut up," Sebastian told him. The warning in his voice was clear.

I wanted to ask what he'd meant by that, but I continued to eat and stay silent.

"Fine. I'm heading out," Wells said, standing up.

The relief that he was leaving came instantly. I didn't much care for his company.

"See what they're saying about the Derby predictions," Storm said to Sebastian, ignoring Wells's announcement.

I watched the large screen as he changed the channel.

"Empire is an early pick," Sebastian told him as they both sat, focused on the men speaking about it.

"Hughes always gets the early pick," Storm replied.

I didn't understand what they were talking about, so I sat back and finished off the pizza, then picked up my water and slowly drank it while the two of them went back and forth about horses and odds.

By the time the sports show they were watching ended, they'd eaten most of the pizza, and Sebastian had refilled my water. I realized, at some point, I had relaxed. I felt comfortable and as if I belonged. Even if I had no idea what they were talking about.

"The sun is setting," Sebastian said, standing up. "Come with me. I want to show you something."

"Okay," I replied, setting my glass back on the table and stand-ing up.

"You think that's smart?" Storm asked.

Sebastian rolled his eyes. "It's a fucking sunset."

The look in Storm's eyes said he didn't agree.

"Ignore him. But we need to hurry before we miss it," Sebastian told me.

I gave him a small nod and then followed him from the room, down toward the main entrance, and outside. The evening breeze was cool, and I wrapped my arms around my chest. Sebastian saw me and frowned.

"Wait here," he said and jogged back into the stables.

I liked seeing the sunset, and from what was said inside, I thought that he must be taking me to see a great view of it. However, I was chilly, and I didn't want to stand out here in this longer than necessary.

Sebastian emerged from the stables then, carrying a hoodie. "Here," he said, coming up to me. "Wear this."

Grateful for some warmth, I took it and pulled it on over my tank top. "Thank you," I said.

"No problem. Now, come this way."

I followed him around the left side of the stables, then between two of the buildings. There was a ladder connected to the structure that looked as if it went to the roof.

"You first. I'll go behind you in case you slip," he said.

I wasn't crazy about heights, but I wasn't scared of them. I thought for a moment, then figured I might as well go on through with this. He'd brought me out here, and it would be rude to refuse to see it.

On the way up, I didn't look down or think about how many feet I was from the ground below. At least I wasn't cold. When I made it to the top, I paused.

"It's okay. I promise," Sebastian told me.

I'd gotten this far. I went ahead and climbed onto the roof and walked far enough back so that Sebastian could join me.

He came up beside me and then touched my arm. "Look," he said, pointing to his right.

I turned, and my breath caught in my throat. It was stunning. There were no trees or buildings blocking the view, and with the mountain in the distance, it looked like a painting.

"It's beautiful," I said.

"Right? I love to see it from up here."

I couldn't remember the last time I'd enjoyed a sunset. Much less one like this. I tucked my hands into the front pockets of the hoodie I was wearing, and we stood there in silence, watching nature's beauty. There was no need for words, and it felt as if talking would be almost irreverent. A show this spectacular deserved one's complete attention.

Seeing something like this reminded me of King. I wanted to watch this with him. But he wasn't here. He was at a party with Scotlin May. My mood began to sour, and I tried very hard to push that thought away.

Had he ever stood here and seen this? I wanted to ask Sebastian, but I decided that remaining silent was best.

Storm was still in the lounge room when we returned. He was standing at the bar, pouring a glass of whiskey. His eyes met mine, and he gave me a tight smile.

Had I done something wrong?

"I'm about to head to the club. You going?" Storm asked, shifting his gaze to Sebastian.

"I don't think we should leave Rumor here alone."

I opened my mouth to tell them I'd go to the room and read, but Storm's gaze locked on me again. He seemed to be studying me hard or thinking it through.

Finally, he sighed. "Yeah. Probably not a good idea."

He walked over to the sofa and sat back down with his drink.

"You're not going?" Sebastian asked him.

Storm glanced back at him. "And leave you here alone with Rumor? No. I think I'll stay."

"What's that supposed to mean?" Sebastian demanded, sounding angry.

Storm picked up the remote control. "It means that I would like to keep you alive."

"Whatever," Sebastian said with annoyance thick in his tone.

I took that moment to interrupt whatever was going to be said next. "I can go upstairs and read. I have several new books."

"Not necessary," Sebastian replied.

"Good idea," Storm said at the exact same time.

Now, this was uncomfortable.

I stepped back and glanced nervously at Sebastian. "I think I should go."

Sebastian shot Storm an annoyed glare. "No. You shouldn't have to stay locked up in that room. He's being dramatic."

"No, I'm not," Storm said with his eyes glued to the screen.

"Yes, he is. Let me make you a drink, and we can find a movie to watch."

I glanced warily over at Storm, who didn't look at either of us.

"Ignore him," Sebastian urged.

I was torn. I didn't want to let my friend down, but then I also didn't want to be somewhere I wasn't welcome. Chewing on my lower lip, I tried to think of a good excuse to leave so that Sebastian was okay with it.

"It's fine. I'm staying. Pop some popcorn or some shit, and I'll find a movie," Storm said, glancing our way once again.

"See," Sebastian said, nudging my arm. "He was just being pissy because he's got a thing for a new dancer at the club and he thinks he can't go because King will be mad if I'm here with you alone."

"I don't have a thing for her," he snapped.

"Yeah, you do."

"If I go read, then you can both go."

"No," they both said in unison.

Confused, I looked at Storm.

He gave me a small smile, as if understanding my confusion. "We leave you alone here, and that would be just as bad as you being here alone with Sebastian."

King hadn't explained this all to me. He hadn't said that my being here was going to make it hard on the others. I should have asked more questions. Thought about the situation.

"Take me to Maeme's," I told them.

Storm let out a sharp laugh. "Fuck no."

I turned to look at Sebastian, who shrugged.

"King comes back, and you're not here?" He shook his head. "He'd lose his shit."

Right now, I wasn't worried about what King would and wouldn't do if I wasn't here. I was frustrated that he'd put me in this position. I didn't like inconveniencing anyone. It gave me extreme anxiety.

"He will be tired from his party tonight," I said bitterly.

Storm laughed again. "Tired of listening to Scotlin's mouth."

Sebastian chuckled beside me, as if he, too, found that funny. Hearing them talk about King not liking Scotlin helped. I was jealous of her. I could admit it. Who wouldn't be?

"He's right. King will want to see you after an evening with her."

I had needed to hear that more than they could ever know. Suddenly, popcorn and a movie sounded perfect.

"Okay then, popcorn and a movie it is."

Storm turned to look back at the television. "You like action, horror, thriller—please do not ask for a chick flick."

I smiled at the thought of making the two of them watch *Bridget Jones's Diary*, but I wouldn't do that to them. I was already keeping them from going to the club, which I was assuming was a strip club from the way they'd talked about it.

"I don't like horror."

"We can work with that," he agreed.

"You ready for me to make you a real drink?" Sebastian asked.

I nodded. I was indeed ready for a cocktail. Even the popcorn sounded appealing.

· TWELVE ·

It wasn't healthy, this thing we were doing.

RUMOR

We were halfway through the second John Wick when I found myself struggling to keep my eyes open. I had thought I could make it through another movie, but I had underestimated the effects of the two drinks Sebastian had made me. Each blink got heavier, and I yawned, then forced myself to sit up. Storm was texting on his phone, and Sebastian was focused on the movie.

I didn't know how much longer it would be before King returned, but I wasn't sure I could wait up any longer. The later it got, the more I began fixating on what it was he was doing.

Before I could say my good nights and excuse myself, the door opened. My stomach did a little flip at the sight of King in a tuxedo. His gaze scanned the room and locked on mine. Smiling, I stood up, happy he was back. That he was looking for me and that I'd get to go to sleep beside him.

I took a step in his direction when his eyes seemed to harden, then flare, as if some demonic presence had taken over him. His hand moved so quickly that I didn't realize what was happening until he had a gun pointed at Sebastian.

"Oh my God," I gasped, moving back and almost falling over the coffee table.

"Take off the goddamn hoodie, Rumor. Now," King demanded, his eyes never leaving Sebastian.

I swung my gaze over to Sebastian as he stood up slowly, then turned to King. Much like King, the movement of his hand was so fast that I almost missed him pulling the pistol from his side and aiming it at King.

My hand flew up to cover my mouth as my heart slammed against my chest.

"NOW!" King shouted. "GET IT OFF!"

I realized he was talking to me, and I reached for the hem of the hoodie while my hands trembled so violently that I was struggling.

"Jesus Christ," Storm said, sounding more put off than anything. "You're scaring the shit out of her."

"He's the one who pulled the gun," Sebastian said, his tone hard. "And over a fucking hoodie. She was cold."

"And you didn't think to let her go get one of mine?" King asked as I pulled the one I was wearing over my head and dropped it onto the sofa. My eyes going back to King.

"We—we—were go-ing outside," I stammered, willing him to look at me and put his gun away. Both of them.

"Were you now?" King asked, his eyes narrowing as he continued to point his gun at Sebastian.

"Fuck this," Storm snarled, standing up. "I stayed here tonight so this shit wouldn't happen. And you're doing it anyway?"

"He put his goddamn hoodie on her," King growled.

"Technically, she put it on herself," Sebastian replied.

"King," I said, willing him to look at me. "Please stop."

His eyes cut toward me then, and I pleaded with him silently. We stood there like that for several moments before he seemed to calm and lower his gun. I put a hand on my stomach, not sure if I was going to throw up or not. Nausea had suddenly come over me, and I wanted to sit back down, but I didn't dare do it.

He put his gun back in the holster under his jacket, then held out a hand to me. "Come here."

My legs felt wobbly as I made my way over to him, checking to be sure Sebastian had also put away his gun. Relieved to see he was no longer pointing it at King, I tried to calm my racing heart as I went to him.

When I was close enough, he grabbed my hand and pulled me to him, then buried his nose in my hair for a second before tucking me under his arm. "Let's go."

I didn't want any more guns or shouting. I went willingly, although the more I thought about what had happened, the angrier I got. He had pointed his pistol at Sebastian over a hoodie? That wasn't sane. It was more like the definition for unstable and unhinged.

None of them said anything more to each other as we left and walked to the stairs, then to King's bedroom. Once inside, he slammed the door with more force than necessary, causing me to jump. I spun around and watched him stalk toward me, which had me backing up away from him until the back of my legs hit the bed. He reminded me of a lion coming after its prey.

"You get cold, sweets, I got a closet full of fucking clothes you can put on."

I nodded, swallowing nervously.

He reached me then, and I held my breath as he ran a hand down my arm.

"No other man's clothing touches this body. Do you understand?"

I didn't, but I nodded anyway. It was just a hoodie. Fabric. It had smelled like laundry detergent. I hadn't even known it was Sebastian's. I'd thought he'd just grabbed the first thing he saw.

"You … you … held a gun on him," I said, fighting the urge to cry or hit him. I was torn between being terrified or pissed off.

He nodded his head once as he ran his knuckles over my collarbone. "Yeah. I should have shot him in the leg to make a point."

I shook my head. "No. It was a hoodie. You don't shoot people over clothing." Words I never thought I'd have to say to someone.

His eyes met mine. "He knew better. Trust me."

I disagreed with him, but I didn't say so.

"I don't like guns," I told him.

He smirked and ran his hand through my curls. "Yeah, but you like me, and I come with a few."

I placed both hands on his chest and tried to move him back. I wanted some personal space. I opened my mouth to tell him so, but then my eyes dropped to the collar of his shirt, and I froze.

Red lipstick was on the starched white cotton. I didn't own red lipstick, and I hadn't been kissing his neck tonight. I shoved hard, and although he didn't move, I felt him tense. His eyes narrowed.

"Get away from me," I bit out.

Fury, pain, betrayal all began to twist in my chest. He'd come in here and held a gun on Sebastian over a piece of clothing, yet he had lipstick on his shirt

"No," he replied, grabbing my hips and pulling me closer to him.

Unable to look at him or his shirt, I glared at the wall to my left. "You have lipstick on your shirt," I snapped as my chest felt like it was going to explode.

His hands tightened their grip on me. "We had to act. Sell the relationship."

"With her lips on you?"

King took my chin between his thumb and forefinger, forcing my face in his direction. I refused to look at him though. I stared at his chest instead.

"Look at me, Rumor," he demanded.

"No! You come back from making out with another woman and pull a gun on your friend for letting me use his hoodie! That is not fair."

King released my chin, but he buried his hands in my hair, holding on to both sides of my head and tilting it back until I had to meet his gaze or close my eyes. "I didn't make out with Scotlin. I endured her. It was fucking hell. One I couldn't wait to get away from. All I thought about was getting back here to you. Then, I walked in and saw you in another man's hoodie. Yeah, I reacted poorly. Rage is a hard bitch, and I had no control over it. I should probably apologize, but I won't because if I ever see another man's clothes on your body again, I will shoot him, I swear to God."

Did I believe him? He hadn't made out with her? Had he kissed her at all? What did it mean that he had to make it believable? How affectionate did they get?

"She put her lips on you," I said.

"I didn't want it. I didn't enjoy it," he replied in a softer tone. "Come take a shower with me."

I shook my head. "We did that earlier." I also wasn't ready to just let this go. Move on. I was considering sleeping on the sofa.

"I want to wash Sebastian's fucking hoodie from your body and Scotlin's shit off me. Please, sweets."

I sighed in frustration at myself. At this situation I had gotten into and the fact that I wanted to please him, even after he pulled a gun on his friend over something so dumb. It wasn't healthy, this thing we were doing. At least not for me. He had too much control over me, and I was the one giving it to him.

Glaring up at him, I clenched my teeth. "Fine. But I want that shirt burned. And the next time you come back with her lipstick on you, I am moving back to Maeme's."

"It'll never happen again. I swear it."

I nodded, feeling somewhat better.

He ran his hand through my hair and wrapped a strand of my curls around one of his fingers. "Are we good?" he asked.

I didn't know if that was the word I would use. But there was no other option, except to just walk away. Demand to go back to Maeme's. Shut him out.

I wouldn't do that though. It would be too painful. The idea of not having him at all was becoming something I couldn't accept. Even if he was unhinged and deranged.

"Yes," I replied.

He leaned down, and his mouth covered mine. One flick of his tongue against my bottom lip, and I opened for him. My body seemed to do its own thing where King was involved. Even if I wanted to put up walls and protect myself, I couldn't. I craved him in ways that would most likely destroy me.

The deep hum of pleasure in his chest vibrated against me. There was one thing I was sure of. King Salazar wanted me. He made that very clear. It was another hold he had on me. No one had ever made me feel this wanted, this desirable. He showed me what it was like to lose myself to pleasure. Perhaps I was going to become addicted to him. Or I already was.

"I want you in the shower, sweets," he said as his hands bunched up the fabric of my tank top until it was over my breasts. "Get naked."

I lifted my arms, and he took it the rest of the way off. Then, he went for his shirt as his eyes locked on my chest.

"Take off the bra."

My hands trembled as I reached behind me to unhook it while he made quick work of his shirt and shrugged out of his jacket. When the lace cups fell free and the bra slid down my arms, he sucked in a breath as an evil smile curled his lips.

"Fuck, I needed that view. Now, get the bottoms off for me and don't wear them again. They're too short."

I paused at the button of my shorts. "Are you serious?"

He tossed the shirt I wanted burned to the ground. "Deadly."

I started to argue when he began to unfasten his pants. My stomach fluttered as his abs flexed and the V cut was fully revealed.

"Naked—now," he ordered, and I remembered what I was doing.

With shaky hands, I finished with my zipper and slid the shorts down my legs, along with my panties, until I could step out of them. When I straightened back up, King's hooded eyes were following my every move. His pants were gone, along with his boxer briefs. My gaze dropped to his rigid erection, and I sucked in a breath at the sight of it.

"Sweets," he said, drawing my attention back to his face, "do you trust me?"

That was a loaded question. There were things I trusted him with, but others I didn't. Not anymore. But we were standing in his room, naked, and I was pretty sure this question meant if I trusted him with my body. That was a yes. He had never *not* rocked my world sexually.

"Yes," I whispered.

"Good girl." The pleasure in his voice curled around me like a warm blanket. He held out his hand to me, and I stepped forward and placed mine in it. "Get on your knees."

I tensed and stared down at his erection again. I'd done this once with Hill. He'd slapped me and told me I was pathetic at it. Panic started to build in my chest. As much as I wanted to put my mouth on him, trace his V cut with my tongue, and worship every ounce of his perfect body, I didn't want to let him down.

He slid his knuckle under my chin and tilted my head back to look up at him. "On your knees," he repeated huskily.

Not wanting to disobey, I slowly eased to my knees in front of him.

He ran his hand over my head. "Damn, that's pretty," he murmured.

Nervously, I reached to wrap my fingers around it. The swollen head was almost blue, I realized. Sticking out my tongue, I ran it over the tip.

King's hand fisted in my hair. "Fuck," he hissed.

I took that as encouragement and licked each side before opening my mouth wide enough to slide it between my lips.

"Fuuuck," he groaned as his hand tightened its hold on my hair. "Such a hot little mouth."

My nipples tingled from his words, and some of my anxiety eased as I took more of him. Wanting to keep making him feel good. Knowing that I was the cause of it. When I had him as deep as I could take him, I lifted my gaze to his, and he let out a deep rumble in his chest.

Our eyes held as I started to work my mouth over him in a steady rhythm.

"Ah, fuck, that's my good girl," he said, staring down at me as if I were some powerful, magical being. I felt like it at the moment.

His legs trembled, and it only urged me on. To take more, give more. Hear his pleasure as it grew.

He jerked hard on my hair, pulling himself free of my mouth. "UP!" he demanded.

I blinked, confused. I thought he'd been enjoying it. What had I done wrong?

"Sweets, if you don't get up and in the shower, I am going to bend you over the bed and fuck the hell out of you."

I wasn't so sure I didn't like that idea. Slowly, I stood, my legs a little wobbly. I looked back at the bed and considered bending over it.

"Don't. Get in the shower," he said. "It's one more door to close off any sounds you make. If they hear you when I'm fucking you and say one goddamn word about it, I can't promise I won't put a bullet in them."

I blinked and sucked in a breath, then decided I had better go get in the shower. I no longer doubted his threat to shoot someone. Not after tonight.

· THIRTEEN ·

You're engaged. Act like it.

KING

The mornings were getting warmer sooner. With a cup of coffee in my hand, I watched as the trainers prepped the thoroughbreds that were leaving today for Louisville. It was a reminder that I would have to pack up and leave in three days myself. With Scotlin. Leaving Rumor here.

I fucking hated it. And I hadn't prepared her for it yet either. The news would cover more than just the horse races. Our engagement would be mentioned, and photos or videos would be posted of the two of us there. I needed to go talk to Maeme about keeping Rumor away from the television while I was gone.

"You cooled down?" Storm asked.

I didn't turn around to look at him. "He knew better."

"Yeah, I know. I should have said something. I thought she'd be in bed when you got back though."

He came to stand beside me, and I glanced over at him to see he had a sausage biscuit in his hand. It smelled good, and I was suddenly hungry. He took a bite and nodded toward the trailers the horses were being put in for travel.

"Sebastian is leaving with them today. That should make you feel better."

I wasn't worried about Rumor wanting Sebastian. She wanted me. She'd made that very clear several times. My concern was hurting her. The hurt that she'd faced already in this life was more than any woman should endure. I didn't want to be another person who broke her or let her down. I just couldn't figure out a way to fix it. Be who she needed.

A darkness settled over me as I thought about it.

"I want the bastard who is stalking Scotlin to make his move. Weed him out and end this bullshit," I said.

"We'd all like that," Storm replied.

My phone started ringing, causing my mood to sour more. No one called me this early unless it was business. I'd left Rumor in the bed to sleep, and I intended to go back up there to her. I didn't need someone calling me away.

Seeing Scotlin's name on my phone didn't help my mood.

"Yeah," I said in greeting, not wanting to deal with whatever this was.

"Good morning," she replied cheerfully. "I need to go shopping today, and you need to go with me."

My grip on the phone in my hand tightened. "I don't fucking shop. You have bodyguards for that shit."

"Don't be a sourpuss this morning. It's a beautiful spring day, and the sun is shining. And I need you because I need your opinion. You are my fiancé after all."

I swear to God, she was fucking mental.

"Fake. I'm your fake fiancé."

She laughed as if I had told her a joke. "That is merely a technicality. We are leaving for the Derby this week. We should be seen out shopping together. I'll be ready at eleven."

"No. I have things to do," I replied sharply, then ended the call.

"Scotlin, I take it?" Storm said.

I nodded and took a drink of my coffee.

"I'd offer to entertain Rumor, but after the shit you pulled last night, I'll pass."

No one was entertaining Rumor but me.

My phone rang again. I wanted to throw the damn thing against the nearest brick wall. Glancing down at it, I saw my father's name. Fucking hell.

"Yeah," I said into the phone.

"You're going shopping."

My head pounded as I glared straight ahead. She'd called my father? Was she fucking serious?

"No, I'm not." My teeth were clenched so tightly that I could hear them grind.

"It's not a request. It's an order."

"Whose fucking order?" I snapped.

I was a grown man, and my father no longer held any power over me. We were equals, and he knew it. Although he often forgot.

"Blaise said you were to be seen with her. That includes shopping. If you make this an issue because of Rumor, then he will move her to Ocala. I wouldn't test him. You want the woman, then fine. Do what you are told. Or else he will remove her from the equation."

"Why? Scotlin has motherfucking bodyguards!" I ground out.

"Because it's what you've been told to do."

"What about the Insantos, who are after Rumor? I thought that was being handled?" I shot back at him.

I was ready for Rumor to be free. So she could live her life. The way she should have always been able to.

"Blaise is dealing with that. He said he would, and once we have the info we need, then we will move. Right now, however, the daughter of the future governor of Georgia is in danger, and you are the one she's supposed to be engaged to. Worry about that."

I inhaled sharply, trying not to lose it. "Rumor has been locked away long enough. I want the Insantos dealt with, or I'll do it myself."

A hard laugh came through the line. "Remember who you are. What we are. Rumor is under our protection because Blaise agreed to help her. We never had to save her. We never had to bring her here. It was her husband we were after. Not her. But we did. She's safe and alive and not being tried for murder because we made sure of it. She's not our priority. We are powerful because of our connections. Who we have in our back pocket. You know this, King. Getting Jefferson in the governor's seat benefits the family. The family always comes first." My father sighed. "Now, Scotlin May is our priority. You're engaged. Act like it."

"Rumor is my priority," I snarled, hating the words coming out of his mouth.

"No. She's not. The family's priority is your priority. Jefferson May is a fucking Republican. When shit starts being dug up about him and the fact that his nineteen-year-old daughter had an abortion comes out, we will need the man who'd knocked her up to be by her side. Showing the voters of Georgia that you are a united front."

"This shit ends once Scotlin's stalker is found. That was what I was told," I reminded him, my chest growing tighter by the moment.

"It ends when Blaise says it does. Not a moment before. Do your job, King."

He ended the call before I could respond.

"FUCK!" I shouted, throwing my phone across the yard and slamming my coffee cup against the fence beside me, causing it to break in two.

"Guess you're going shopping," Storm said beside me.

I turned and stalked back to the stables without responding. Right now, I needed Rumor. She was the only thing that could ease the violence pumping through my veins.

· FOURTEEN ·

This puts a spin on things.

RUMOR

It was strange how the light of a new day seemed to make everything seem brighter. The darkness faded away so easily. You could accept the things you'd never imagined you would. Like the fact that the man you loved had held a gun on his friend over a hoodie.

Standing in front of the mirror, I worked a comb through my unruly curls and looked at the woman staring back at me. She was different and not just because there was no bruise she was hiding or fear curling in her chest at what the day would bring. The woman was happy. As messed up as it all was, when I really thought about it, I wouldn't want to be anywhere else.

King filled every void that had haunted me my entire life. He made me feel wanted, special, as if I belonged. I felt … needed. Cherished even. Violence had shattered me once. I'd even believed it had taken my soul. Which made the fact that the man to save me, heal me, was more violent than Hill had ever been.

"I was hoping you'd still be in bed."

King's voice startled me, and I spun around to see him leaning against the doorway of the bathroom. I wondered if the sight of him would always affect me like this. The way his smile captivated me. It took all other thoughts away and replaced them with him. He was my happy place.

"You weren't there," I replied, returning his smile.

"My mistake," he said, shoving off from his relaxed stance and walking over to me. "I left so that you could rest. If I had stayed, I'd have woken you up with my head between your legs." He slid a hand around my waist and pressed his palm against my back, gently nudging me closer. "I've had my coffee, but I was coming back for my meal."

A laugh fell from my lips as I tilted my head back to look up at him. "I don't see any food."

He brushed the pad of his thumb over my mouth. "I'd be happy to show you where it is."

A sigh of pleasure escaped me, and he smirked as he continued to caress different areas. My cheekbones, jawline, the side of my neck. He seemed lost in deep thought as he silently went about touching me with reverence. I trembled slightly as I stood there, watching him.

"Are you cold?" he asked in a low voice just above a whisper.

I shook my head. This had absolutely nothing to do with being cold and everything to do with him.

"You're not scared of me, are you, sweets?"

"No," I whispered.

He cupped my face as his gaze seemed to sink into me. As if he were trying to see all my thoughts. Find my darkest secrets. "Not even a little?"

I shook my head, but remained silent.

"I'd kill anyone who hurt you."

I knew this already, and as horrifying as it sounded, my body seemed to like it. A little too much.

"Anyone who touched you," he added.

I considered asking for clarification on that one and decided against it. I might not want to hear the answer to it. Accepting who King was and loving him anyway was something I had already worked through. Seemed I couldn't stop loving him. Even if he did things like pulling a gun on someone for letting me wear their hoodie.

"I have to leave you this weekend. I don't want to."

Even as he said it, I already knew where he was going. It was impossible to live here and not know that the Kentucky Derby was coming up.

"I want you to stay with Maeme."

I nodded, not wanting to speak. I didn't want him to hear the disappointment in my voice. He was going to be with Scotlin. Thinking about it and her red lipstick put a damper on the joy I'd been feeling.

"When will you leave?" I asked.

He looked as unhappy about it as I felt. That helped a little. He didn't want Scotlin. I might not trust him completely because there would always be things he couldn't tell me. But it was hard not to believe him when he said he didn't want her. She'd hurt him in the past. That was something that would always stand between them.

"Thursday," he replied.

"And you'll be back Sunday?" I asked, needing to prepare myself for his absence.

"Monday."

I hadn't realized it would be that long. My heart sank even more. It wasn't fair to make him feel bad about it. This was his world. His job. It wasn't his fault that a gang was looking for me and I had to stay hidden. He hadn't been the one to put me in danger. Hill had.

"I'll read a lot of books," I told him, trying my best to smile. "I won't even notice you're gone."

A grin tugged at his lips. "Don't go that far. I can't shoot a library for taking my place. And if I burned it down, Maeme would never let me have her banana pudding again."

The laugh that came from me eased some of the ache. The corners of his eyes crinkled as his smile spread across his handsome face. The blue of his irises seemed brighter.

"I'll miss you, I promise," I assured him.

His grip on me tightened. "I wouldn't go if I didn't have to. They aren't giving me a choice."

"I know."

"It'll be over soon, I swear."

I nodded. I hoped so. I was ready to be rid of Scotlin May.

King had eaten breakfast at Maeme's with me, then left to go handle business—whatever that was today. He never shared the details, and that was part of his life I realized I had no choice but to accept. Once he was gone, I visited with Maeme for a while, then escaped to her library to find books for this weekend and get my mind off the details I didn't know that were starting to torture me. Like where King was going to sleep. Would he be sharing a room with Scotlin? I knew he wouldn't share a bed, but how far would he go to sell this engagement?

For the first time in my life, books didn't distract me. Figured when I needed it the most, it wasn't strong enough. I was being haunted by thoughts of what could happen with King and Scotlin. The idea of her touching him made me want to curl up and weep. In fact, I had found myself tearing up several times. I didn't cry often. It was something I had fought against so hard that I wondered if I had broken that reaction inside me. At least until today.

Wiping at the current tear rolling down my face, I growled, frustrated with myself. I was in a room full of books, and I was thinking about stuff I had no control over. I'd done this to myself. Falling in love with King Salazar was the most reckless, insane, confusing thing I had ever done. Yet I wouldn't change it.

The door opened behind me, and I turned to see Maeme. She smiled at me, but I saw the concern in her eyes. Stupid tears. I wanted to go back to not being able to cry.

"Dr. Drew is here," she told me.

I frowned. "Why? His last visit, he said my ribs were fine."

"Your birth control. He said according to the dates you gave him, it was time for your next one."

Oh. I hadn't even thought about that. Thank God he had.

I set the book down on the table. "Yes. Okay," I replied, making my way to the doorway to meet her.

She touched my arm gently. "Are you okay?"

Just the slightest bit of affection had me wanting to burst into tears and wail like a baby. I swallowed it down though and fought against the emotion clawing at my throat.

"I'm fine," I assured her. "Emotional book."

My lie didn't work. I could see it in her all-too-knowing eyes. But she didn't call me out on it. Instead, she gave me a nod and turned to lead me to the back staircase that I knew went down to the basement, where there was a complete doctor's office set up for the Mafia's private doctor who made house visits.

When we reached the bottom of the stairs, Dr. Drew was standing in the middle of the now-familiar white room and sterile-looking environment. He was texting something on his phone when he glanced up and smiled at me.

"Good afternoon," he said brightly, tucking his phone into his coat pocket. "You look even better than the last time I saw you. I see they are taking good care of you."

"Yes," I agreed.

"I never doubted otherwise. When Maeme takes someone under her wing, then they always flourish," he said, nodding his head at her in appreciation.

"I can't take the credit this time. King had more to do with it than I did. He doesn't let anyone get too close to her these days."

Dr. Drew's eyes widened in surprise. "Well, that's a turn of events."

I smiled, feeling my face heat up.

"All right, this should be routine for you. Since I'm not the OB/GYN you regularly saw and I don't know your history, I need to do an examination. Just to make sure all is well. Then, we will move forward with your shot. When was your last Pap smear?"

Oh God. Not that. I hadn't been told I was having a gyno checkup. Dread sank over me. "Right before I got married, so …" I paused to count the time since my wedding to Hill. "Uh, seventeen months now."

"You are definitely due for one of those too. Let's start with the urine sample," he said. "This way." He headed for the room opposite the one I had been in before to have X-rays of my ribs done.

"I'll wait out here," Maeme said. "Unless you'd prefer me in there."

The less people who had to see my vagina, the better.

"No. It's fine."

Dr. Drew handed me a collection cup with the cleansing cloth packet. "Bathroom is that door right down there to the left."

I tried to think about King and this morning to get my mind off the exam. Thankfully, I had drunk enough water this morning that peeing on cue wasn't a problem. Walking my collection of urine back into the exam room wasn't enjoyable, but it had to be done. I needed that shot. King hadn't used a condom with me in weeks. Since the second day we'd started having sex, to be exact.

Dr. Drew took the cup and went over to his workstation and put the strips in it before turning back to me. "I've got you a gown laid out. Slip off your clothes and get it on. I'll be back shortly."

Once he closed the door behind him, I began undressing. I'd be done soon and back in the library. Free from examinations for another year. The positive spin was, I didn't have to leave the house to go have it done. I tried to focus on that while I changed into my gown and sat down on the exam table.

"Are you ready?" Dr. Drew called through the door.

I adjusted the gown to make sure all my parts were covered. Not that it mattered really since he'd be looking between my legs soon.

"Yes," I replied.

I took a deep breath as he walked back into the room. This was not a big deal. I was a grown woman. I was being silly. I forced a smile as he walked over to my urine sample.

The silence in the room felt awkward, so I tried to think of something to say just to make myself feel better. But what did one say to a man currently studying your pee? Dropping my gaze to my hands clasped in my lap, I decided to wait and let him speak first.

He cleared his throat, and I glanced up to see him turn around with both his hands stuck in the pockets of his slacks. When his eyes met mine, there was a serious expression on his face. I stilled.

What had my urine told him? He wasn't easing my nerves over the exam he had to do. Where was his smile? Wasn't he supposed to be making me feel better about this?

He glanced back at the door, then walked over to it and closed it softly. Perhaps he felt weird about having to give me a Pap smear. He'd be up close and personal with my lady bits. Maybe I should have had Maeme come in here. I could still ask.

"Rumor." He said my name just above a whisper. That was odd and not helping my growing anxiety.

"Yes?" I replied, wishing he would stop with this strange behavior.

I wanted the door back open. Maeme should be in here. I didn't know Dr. Drew that well after all. Nurses were normally in the room with doctors.

"You're pregnant."

I sat there, staring at him. All other thoughts suddenly snatched from my head.

"What?" I asked, my voice cracking as those two words slowly sank in.

"The urine sample. You're pregnant," he repeated. "I don't know how far along, and I don't have the equipment here to do an ultrasound." He ran a hand over his head and sighed. "I should have tested you before the X-rays on your ribs. You said you were on the shot, so I assumed you were safe. It's rare that someone can get pregnant taking the Depo-Provera shot. We will need to run tests. See how far along you are. Do you remember the last time you had sex with, uh"—he paused—"your former husband?"

I couldn't speak. I had no words. I just sat there, not knowing what I felt.

"I know this is a lot to take in, and I am sorry. Perhaps an examination would be the best way to start this. I can get an idea of how far along you are by checking for changes in your uterus and cervix. It isn't accurate, but it will give us a ballpark. If you could tell me the last time you had sex, then that, too, would help."

I blinked as I looked back at him. That was a very easy answer. However, the last time I'd had sex with Hill, I didn't know. Sex with him had become something rare toward the end.

"Sex? Or ... sex with Hill?" I asked, too numb to even be embarrassed by this question.

His eyes widened slightly. "You've had sex since you left your ... Hill?"

I nodded.

"I need to know when."

I dropped my gaze to my lap. "Last night."

He was silent for a moment, and I began to twist the gown I was wearing in my hands.

"Was that the first time?"

I shook my head, not looking up at him.

"When was?"

I swallowed hard, feeling nausea slowly creep in. "Five ... almost six weeks ago."

"Were there other times in between?"

I nodded.

He let out a heavy sigh. "King."

I nodded again.

"I see. This puts a spin on things. Let's put that aside right now and have you lie back."

I took a deep breath as a cold sweat broke out over my body and my hands began to feel clammy. I did as he'd instructed and closed my eyes tightly as he put my feet in the stirrups and moved my gown up to my thighs.

How was this happening? I knew that I hadn't been positive about the date of my last shot, but I'd been close.

This wasn't Hill's baby. That much I knew. It had been over two, maybe even three, months since we'd had sex, and even then, he hadn't come inside me. He had thought it was messy and didn't like it.

But … what would King say … what would he do when he found out?

I'd told him I was on birth control. He'd made sure of it. He had asked me. I was still in danger from a gang. I couldn't be pregnant. What kind of life would I be bringing my baby into?

My baby.

Those two words hit me like a sledgehammer, and I covered my mouth to keep from letting out a sob. I had a baby growing inside me. A life that was a part of me. That I had helped create.

"Easy. Relax," Dr. Drew said as I felt him reach inside me and probe around.

I sucked in a breath as a tear squeezed out of the corner of my eye and rolled down the side of my face.

"It's very early," he said. "I'd say six weeks, at the most."

My eyes flew open. "How? I didn't have sex six weeks ago. I said it was *almost* six weeks. Closer to five."

He nodded and removed his fingers from inside of me. "Yes, but in pregnancy, we count from the last menstrual cycle, which you didn't have since you were on the shot. Technically, the embryo started growing around three weeks ago. Meaning it was fertilized shortly before. Even if you had incorrectly guessed how long it had been since your last shot, it's not one hundred percent effective."

He reached for my gown and pulled it back down, then took my hand and helped me sit back up. When his eyes met mine, I could see the concern in them, and I felt my own start to water up again. I seemed to be doing a lot of that today.

"I understand that by law, I can't tell anyone, but you have to understand that your situation … my situation is different. I don't fear the government the way I do lying to anyone in the family.

They are the only law that exists for those of us involved with them. That means me … and now you."

He was telling me I had to tell King or he would.

Words didn't come to me. I simply nodded.

"I'll go get Maeme." His tone was gentle, but I could hear the warning there. To be prepared.

I stared straight ahead at the wall while he went to get her. There was a child inside me. King's baby. And as much as I loved him, I knew it wasn't enough to make him love me.

What if he didn't want it? What if he asked me to abort it? He wasn't young, like he had been with Scotlin. He was older. He was changed.

Life had changed him.

"Lord, Drew, she's white as a ghost," Maeme said as she walked into the room. "What on earth did you do to her?" The fierceness in her tone was almost frightening.

I turned my gaze to her, and I knew he hadn't told her yet. I had hoped he would. Get it over with. Just say it.

"Rumor." He said my name with a nudge to his tone.

The tightening on my throat didn't make it easy to speak. "I'm …" I whispered, but I had to stop and suck in some air.

It felt as if I wasn't getting enough oxygen all of a sudden. The room started to spin, and I gripped the sides of the examination table and tried to force air into my lungs. I could hear the accelerated beat of my heart in my ears. A darkness was closing in on my peripheral vision, and I fought harder to breathe. Nothing helped though.

"Get her!" Maeme yelled just before the darkness pulled me under.

· FIFTEEN ·

I'm just trying to protect King.

RUMOR

A cold, damp cloth was pressed against my head and cheeks. My lungs no longer burned, and I was lying down. I tried to remember where I was before opening my eyes because I was clearly not alone. Someone was moving the cloth around my face gently.

"He can't know. No one can. At least not right now. There is too much at stake," I heard Maeme speak above me.

"You think it's smart to keep this from him?" Dr. Drew's voice sounded unsure.

"Yes. For now. I know, and that is all she needs. I can take care of her. Make sure she and my great-grandbaby are okay. There are issues that have to be dealt with first. If King knows, then he will act irrationally. Mess up. Get himself killed. This baby needs its father."

"Very well. It's your call. You'd better keep me alive when the time comes."

She wasn't going to tell King. I lay there, trying to decide if I was relieved or not. Did I want him to know? Could I keep this a secret from him? How would he get himself killed?

"You are safe. This is my call, and I will take full responsibility."

"You'll tell Blaise?" It was a question, not a demand.

Maeme sighed. "Yes. I'll have to. But he will agree with me. Hopefully, he'll move the Insantos bullshit to the top of his priority list when he finds out."

I opened my eyes then and stared up at Maeme beside me, taking the cloth from my face. Her eyes met mine.

"There she is," she said softly. "You had too much to take in at one time. Couldn't handle it all. But you're fine. You are going to stay that way too. I'm gonna take care of you."

My hand moved to my stomach. It was still flat, and that made it even harder to believe there was a child inside of me. A living being that was part of me.

"The baby is just fine too," Maeme said, patting the top of my hand gently. "Just lie there and relax. Take deep breaths. You are going to be okay. I'm not gonna let anything happen to you or my great-grandbaby."

That lump of emotion began growing in my throat again.

"You're not going to tell King," I said, wanting to clarify what I had heard.

She squeezed my hand in hers. "Not right away. He needs to stay focused. What he is dealing with right now is dangerous, and if his head isn't in the game, he could get hurt. Or killed. Neither of us wants that."

"I'll leave you two to talk. But the vitamins we discussed are right here," Dr. Drew told Maeme. "I'll be back in a week to check on her, and I'll get the ultrasound machine moved in this weekend while King is gone."

"Thank you, Drew," she replied. "We are just fine."

"I'd go over what all she needs to eat and what to do to take care of her and the baby, but I figure you've got that handled."

"That I do." Maeme's bright tone didn't match her expression. The worry lines in her face were hard to mask.

I wanted to be alone. Back at the cottage. I needed time to think this all through. There were so many questions and fears running through my head. I didn't know where to even start.

Dr. Drew gave me an encouraging smile. "I leave you in good hands."

I managed a nod, but nothing more.

"Now, let's sit you up slowly and move you to a more comfortable location," Maeme suggested.

"I had alcohol last night," I told her as the thought hit me.

She took my hand and pulled me up to a sitting position again. "Won't hurt a thing. Most women have a few drinks before they find out their pregnant. You're early still. The baby didn't get any of it."

That was a small relief among the list of things I had to worry about.

"Now, we are gonna go up to the sunroom. I'll bring you a cup of peppermint tea, and you can read a book and relax."

I wasn't going to be able to focus on a book, but I stood up and let her lead me up the stairs anyway. Perhaps while I pretended to read, I could think about what would happen next. How I would move forward. What I would tell King when the time came.

I just wished I knew how he was going to react.

The sunroom was warm, and the view of Maeme's backyard with all the flowers in bloom would normally be a cozy, welcome spot. The book in my lap remained unread, although it lay open. Thankfully, Maeme had left me alone with my thoughts.

I stared out at the azaleas, Spanish bluebells, and tulips. My hand kept finding its way to my stomach. The reality seemed to be even too much for me to comprehend. The longer I sat and let this sink in, the more I found that I wanted the baby. Even if King didn't, I did. I loved this baby, and how odd that was. To love something you'd never seen and just found out existed. It was strange and powerful. I looked down at my hand covering where the tiny baby was now growing.

Even with all the fear and uncertainty, a small trickle of joy was finding its way inside. Slowly taking over all else. I hadn't planned this, but now that it was here, I wanted it. Possibly more than I wanted anything else.

The sound of Maeme's footsteps got my attention, and I moved my hand from my stomach and turned several pages in the book before she appeared. I didn't want her to think I was in here worrying. I couldn't explain what I was currently going through, and feeling as if I had to stressed me out.

"I brought lunch," Maeme said as she entered the sunroom.

I glanced up from the book in my lap to see her carrying a tray.

"I could have come to the kitchen to eat," I told her, closing the book and setting it on the table beside me.

"You've had a lot to take in today. You need to relax," she informed me, placing the tray down in front of me.

There was pasta salad with cucumbers, which I loved, fresh mixed berries, and what looked like chicken salad inside a croissant.

"Did you like the tea? I have some more that will be safe for you to drink if you'd like to try another."

I shook my head. "The water is fine. Thank you. This looks amazing," I replied.

"I've got to make sure you eat properly," she said, giving me a pointed look.

I hoped that didn't mean she was planning on keeping me here. Not that I didn't enjoy her home, but I wanted to go back to King. He'd want me back with him too. There would be no explanation that she could give him to change that.

"I reckon King will be back soon," she said, taking the seat across from me.

I reached for the tray and set it in my lap. "He didn't say where he was going or for how long," I told her.

"He leaves in a few days, as you know. If he thinks something is off with you, we might have a problem with him leaving. He has to go, Rumor. This is vitally important to us. If he knows you're pregnant, he won't leave."

I wasn't so sure. I picked up a strawberry and took a bite, simply nodding. I didn't know what she wanted me to say.

"I don't want you to feel alone in this. I'm just trying to protect King. He's a hothead, and if he thinks he has to choose, he'll choose you and the baby. That could get him killed. In our world, the family comes first, and that's not necessarily the biological one. We will get this Scotlin May thing behind us, handle the Insantos, and when you bring my great-grandchild into this world, all will be well. I just need you to trust me."

Trust with this family was a touchy subject. I trusted them to keep me safe, but I also knew there was so much I didn't know. They would lie to me if they felt they needed to. I would never get the complete truth.

"Okay," I replied, knowing I could say nothing else.

"Good," she said, smiling and standing back up. "Now, I will leave you to eat in peace and enjoy your book."

"Thanks again for lunch," I told her.

Her smile was genuine and warm. That I could trust.

· SIXTEEN ·

You're crazy.

KING

Rumor was upset. I could tell she was trying to hide it, but she wasn't doing a good job at it. I reached for the bottle of whiskey and poured more than two fingers into a glass. Listening to Scotlin talk for hours and try on clothes had been fucking miserable. All I had wanted to do was get back to Rumor, but she had been stand-offish since I'd picked her up from Maeme's.

"Already drinking heavy in the afternoon." Thatcher's amused drawl came from the doorway.

I took a drink and turned around. "I thought you'd left for Louisville already," I said.

"Nope. I'm staying behind. We can't all go running off."

If only I could be the one staying behind.

"Want to trade places?"

He chuckled and walked over to pour his own glass. "What? And rob you of some good quality time with Scotlin?"

I grimaced and took another drink. "Nothing good or quality about it."

Thatcher took his glass that he'd filled over halfway and smirked at me. "It can't be that bad. Scotlin was the first bitch that let you tie her up with your rope and spank her like a bad girl. I remember when you were so enamored with her that you couldn't keep your dick out of her."

I opened my mouth to tell him that wasn't how it had been, not even close, when my eyes caught on Rumor standing in the doorway. She was pale.

Motherfucker! Why did they always say shit like this? They knew she was here.

I set my glass down and went directly to her.

Why was she so goddamn pale? Had what he said upset her that much?

"He's full of shit, sweets," I said as I reached her.

She gave me a weak smile and nodded.

"It was fucking forever ago," Thatcher said, surprising me. He never cared about covering his messes. "He's taken a whip to so many hot asses since hers that he couldn't pick it out of a lineup."

And there it was. Thatcher being a jackass.

"Ignore him," I told her, then cupped the side of her face in my hand. "Are you okay?"

She looked like she might faint, and my chest felt fucking weird. I didn't like seeing her this way.

"I'm fine. Just thirsty," she said. "I should have stayed upstairs."

"No," I said, shaking my head. "You're not a prisoner in that room. You wanted a bath, and I left you alone so I wouldn't get in there with you."

Another smile that didn't reach her eyes.

"What do you want to drink?" I asked her. "I'm day drinking. Want to join me?"

She shook her head. "Just water or maybe some juice."

"What kind of juice, sweets? I think all we have is cranberry. Don't usually keep juice in here, but I can get some from the main house."

"Water is fine."

Something wasn't right. I just needed her to tell me what it was, and I'd fix it.

"You sure you're okay?"

She nodded again.

She was lying, but I couldn't force it out of her. I had to find a way to get her to talk. Or either ask Maeme if she'd said anything to her about Scotlin. Did she know I'd been shopping with her today? Was that it? Fucking hell. I needed this shit to end.

"You hungry?" I asked.

She didn't respond right away, then finally shook her head. Her color wasn't getting better, and I was getting concerned. Was she sick and didn't want to tell me?

"Come on," I said, nodding my head toward the kitchen area. "Let's get you some water. You can look and see if any of the food that Minna dropped off today looks good to you."

"As much fun as it is watching you hover over her like a momma hen, I got shit to do," Thatcher said, setting his empty glass on the bar. "Don't suffocate her too much."

I ignored him as he walked past us to leave. With him gone, I could ask more specific questions and hopefully get her to talk. I went to get her some ice water, then placed it on the bar in front of her before taking her chin and looking her in the eyes.

"You don't feel well, or something is bothering you. Whatever it is, tell me."

She blinked, but said nothing as she stared up at me.

"Sweets," I said sternly, but not enough to scare her.

"I don't feel great," she said just above a whisper.

"I'll call Drew," I told her, dropping my hold on her chin and reaching for my phone.

"NO!" Her hand shot out and grabbed my wrist.

I stared at her, confused.

"He gave me my ... he stopped by today. I was due for a checkup. I'm fine. Just a bug or something."

Maeme hadn't said anything about a checkup. That was odd. Why was I just now hearing about it?

"What kind of checkup?" I asked.

"The … woman kind," she replied, and some color came back to her cheeks.

I stilled. "What do you mean, the woman kind?"

She took in a deep breath, as if she was exasperated with my questioning. "You know, the kind a woman has done once a year. I was overdue."

My nostrils flared as I inhaled sharply, jamming my phone into my pocket. "Tell me what he did," I demanded.

Her eyes widened. "You want details?"

My teeth were clenched so tightly that I wasn't sure I could open them to speak. I nodded.

"A Pap smear, okay?" she said.

No, he fucking didn't. I moved past her, stalking toward the door. I hadn't been told Drew was going to lay her on a goddamn table and open her legs.

"KING!" she cried out, and I paused, trying to get control of the rage rolling through me like a tidal wave.

She had set her glass down and was rushing after me. "Where are you going?" she asked.

"To kill a man," I replied honestly.

She grabbed my arm so tightly that her nails bit into my skin. "NO! Who?"

My eyes dropped to her tiny hand that held on to my biceps as if she had the strength to stop me. "The doctor."

"What?!"

I lifted my gaze back to hers, trying to will myself to calm down, but the image of her lying on a table with her legs open in front of him was fucking with my head.

"No man …" I said, holding her gaze. "NO MAN looks at or touches what is mine."

The panic on her face was the only thing keeping me grounded.

"King, it is normal. Women go to the doctor. It's for my health and to make sure I'm okay. I needed a checkup."

I shoved my fingers in her curls and fisted the caramel locks in my hand. "Then, a woman doctor can do it."

She let out a sigh and closed her eyes for a minute. The pale color was back, and I was torn between picking her up and carrying her up the stairs or going to find Doc D and ending his life.

"It's fine. Maeme was there. He kept me covered with a gown. It was quick and over. Please, don't go. I don't want you to leave."

Fuck. I took several deep breaths and kept my eyes on her as I fought off the need to murder. He'd still touched her. Been where no one belonged but me. I stood there, staring at her as she watched me, waiting for my next move.

Mine. I'd claimed her without thinking. Called her mine. I wanted to see Doc D bleed out because he had touched her. This wasn't me, and it wasn't like anything I'd experienced before. The painful grip on my chest, the insane possessiveness.

"Okay," I said, knowing I couldn't leave her after she begged me not to.

I wasn't sure I could do anything she didn't want me to do. That was … eye-opening.

Her grip on me eased, and she rubbed where she had been holding on to me so tightly. "Thank you."

The tightness in my chest wasn't letting go though.

Then, she laughed. A soft, musical sound that felt like a balm over the monster that had possessed me. Calming him.

"Why are you laughing?" I asked, unable to keep the smile from spreading across my face.

How was it that she controlled my mood?

"You were going to kill a doctor for giving me a much-needed checkup," she said, then shook her head. "You're crazy."

Her color was back. The rest of the tension inside me eased. She was okay.

"I thought you'd already established that," I said. "Last night."

She laughed again and then gave me the sweetest fucking smile in the world. "Yes, I guess I did."

Backing her up until her back hit the wall, I caged her in. "I'm gonna need to make sure I stake my claim now. Remind you who you belong to."

She pulled her bottom lip between her teeth. I reached up and tugged it free before lowering my head and covering those full, pouty lips with mine.

SEVENTEEN

*Y'all might come in different wrapping, but inside, you're all the same.
Smart, calculating, and you wield your pussy like a weapon.*

RUMOR

She was the first girl he'd tied up and whipped. That kept replaying in my head.

Even with his arm around me as he slept, I stared at the wall, unable to do the same. He would be leaving with her in two days, and since yesterday, when I'd overheard Thatcher talking about Scotlin being King's first and him not being able to keep his dick out of her, I had felt dread slowly seeping in.

What if she offered it to him this weekend? He wanted it. He craved it, yet he never asked me to go to the tack room. Now … well, now, even if he asked me, I'd have to say no because I had another life in me to think about. When what we were doing started to bore him and he went back to his different women and his kink, I'd be left with our baby. My baby.

I tried to close my eyes and shove it all from my mind, but it was proving impossible. I needed to focus on the good. Not the bad or the what-ifs. I had money. Maeme had said I had a lot of money. When the Insantos were no longer after me, I'd be free to live life normally. I wouldn't struggle to pay the bills, and I could give my baby a safe, comfortable home. I could love him or her enough for both of us if King chose not to be involved. Regardless, I'd have my own family. I'd have a child to love, take care of, raise. It wasn't all bad. I had to remember that.

A phone rang, breaking the silence, and I jumped, startled. King tensed, then released me to sit up and reach for his cell beside the bed. I rolled onto my back, watching him as the screen lit up, illuminating his face. He took my breath away. My chest ached at the sight of him. I loved him. I had his child inside of me. That was more than I had ever had before. This wasn't bad, considering the things I'd faced and overcome before him.

"Yeah? Okay, my dad will be there. Shit. Fine."

He dropped the phone down onto the bed and muttered, "Fuuuck," while rubbing his face with a hand before turning to look at me.

"Is something wrong?" I asked.

His scowl softened. "The alarm system outside the perimeter of my house went off. Scotlin is there and freaking out. My father is on his way, but I have to go meet them."

Scotlin. I was beginning to hate that name. I swallowed the emotion suddenly clogging my throat. Was my new brink-of-tears reaction something that came with pregnancy? I didn't like it. Making myself vulnerable and showing that vulnerability were two different things. The former I could normally hide well.

King leaned down and pressed a kiss to my mouth, then brushed some hair back from my face. "I'll be back as soon as I can. You're safe here. I'll have Thatch come sleep in the room next door, and no one can get onto this property without permission and live for very long."

I nodded, afraid my voice would crack if I tried to speak.

He climbed out of bed, and I turned back to face the wall, not wanting to see him get dressed and leave. Saving Scotlin seemed to be his number one job these days. What if it didn't end soon? The more they were together like this, the more likely they'd rekindle their feelings for one another.

Pulling the blankets up to my chin, I closed my eyes again and tried to pretend I wasn't upset over his leaving. Being clingy wasn't going to encourage him to want to stay with me. He needed space, and I had to be understanding and patient if I was going to have a chance at keeping him. Although that chance was starting to look slimmer by the day. I couldn't be sure he wouldn't sleep with her in Kentucky. I realized she could give him all the things I wouldn't. She wasn't damaged goods.

As I stood over the sink, brushing my teeth, a cold sweat slowly eased over me, and I paused, taking the toothbrush from my mouth. I spit, then stared at myself for a brief second before turning and running to the toilet. With just enough time to drop to my knees and grab the seat before the first heave hit me.

My eyes watered, and I tried to hold back my hair, but I failed at it mostly. When I was done, I flushed, then sat back, leaning against the wall. I held my head in my hands and rested it on my bent knees.

Why did I still feel nauseous? Wasn't that feeling supposed to leave once you threw up? I didn't move, afraid I would need to vomit again even though there was nothing left to come up. Dry-heaving was horrible, and I didn't want to go through that.

Wasn't it bad enough that I'd woken up alone? King hadn't come back last night. Irrational thoughts of him getting in bed with Scotlin and holding her tortured me. Although I didn't think he'd do that to me. Would he? No. He wouldn't. I had to believe that. Maybe she had just been scared, and he'd slept in another room.

Lifting my head, I looked at the toilet, then laid my head back against the wall. I needed a shower now. I was sure I'd gotten vomit in my hair. I could smell its sour stench. That scent was going to make me puke again. I had to get rid of it. With a sigh, I stood up and walked over to the shower to turn it on, then began to undress while the water heated.

I'd like to think I had a stomach virus, but I'd read enough books. I knew this was the beginning of morning sickness. How long did this last? Could I take something to stop it? I needed a book about pregnancy. I'd have to ask Maeme to get me one. I knew so little about it.

The steam coming from the shower caused me to pause. Was hot water bad for the baby? Why hadn't I asked more questions when I found out? I literally knew nothing.

Reaching in, I turned the heat down some until it was more warm than hot, then stepped inside. I sighed with relief as the water ran over me and seemed to refresh me from my moment of yuck. I wasn't going to be able to hide this from King. If he had been here, he would have witnessed my getting sick. I couldn't very well say it was a stomach virus if it lasted for weeks. He would know. I had to go see Maeme as soon as I got dressed.

I quickly washed my hair and cleaned my body. Getting out of here before King returned was the only way I was getting to talk to her alone. He'd go with me if he got back first. I skipped drying my hair and got dressed before hesitantly brushing my teeth again. Thankfully, it didn't send me running to the toilet this time.

My stomach growled as I started out the door of the bedroom. Frowning, I looked down at it. How was I hungry after I just puked up my guts? The thought of waffles with berries and bacon made my mouth water. It wasn't Sunday, so there wouldn't be any waffles at Maeme's, but perhaps I could ask her for some. Would that be bad?

Just as I passed the open door to the lounge, I heard noise and stepped back. Was King here? He'd stop me or go with me if he saw me. I waited and listened, but whoever it was had gotten quiet. Easing up enough to peek inside, I saw Thatcher holding a coffee mug with a cigarette hanging out of his mouth.

"You need something?" he asked, not looking up from his phone.

I didn't say anything, not sure he was talking to me. He hadn't actually put his eyes on me. Maybe he was talking on speakerphone.

He lifted his head then and locked his gaze on me, then took the cigarette from his mouth. "Do you?" he asked.

I walked fully into view then and managed a smile. The man made me nervous.

"Uh, no. I was … I just didn't want to bother you."

He took a drink of his coffee as he studied me.

"I, uh … I was going to Maeme's."

He put the cigarette back between his teeth, then started in my direction. "All right."

I stood there, unsure if that was the end of our conversation or not.

He walked past me. "You coming or not?"

Coming? With him? No, that would not work.

"What?" I asked, stalling.

He sighed heavily, then turned back around and looked at me. "You can't walk to Maeme's alone. I'll drive you over."

Okay, that wasn't a completely bad thing. I'd get there a lot quicker and have time with her before King showed up. I doubted Thatcher was going to stay and visit.

"Oh, um, thank you," I replied.

He turned back around, and I followed him outside into the warm morning air, then toward a black SUV parked closest to the barn. I watched him toss his cigarette onto the ground and put it out with his boot. At least I wouldn't have to worry about the secondhand smoke. I was pretty sure that was bad for the baby. He didn't open my car door, but I hadn't expected him to. I was just so used to King, Sebastian, and Storm doing it. I thought maybe that was a thing with these men.

Once we were inside, Thatcher said little as he backed up and turned the vehicle toward the exit. My hands fidgeted in my lap nervously, and I kept my eyes on the road. Being alone with this man wasn't something I had ever planned on doing, but I could survive it to get to Maeme's.

"You pissed he didn't come back?" Thatcher asked, breaking the silence.

I glanced at him. He had one hand on the steering wheel, and the other still held his mug as he rested it on his thigh.

"No."

He smirked, not looking over at me. "Don't believe you. You're running off. Knowing when he gets back and you're gone, he'll act stupid."

"No, that's not what I'm doing. I wanted to go get a book and see Maeme. That's it."

He turned his gaze toward me and narrowed his eyes, then let out a deep chuckle that verged on evil. "Yeah. Sure. Y'all might come in different wrapping, but inside, you're all the same. Smart, calculating, and you wield your pussy like a weapon."

I wanted to set him straight, but then I didn't trust him. He was dangerous in a way the others weren't. Sure, they all killed people and did questionable things, but this one, I was pretty sure he'd kill for sport and then smoke a cigarette over the bleeding corpse.

Relieved at the sight of Maeme's house, I decided to keep my mouth shut. He pulled up to the walkway and stopped the SUV.

"Thank you," I said, reaching for the handle.

"Don't fuck with his head, yeah?"

I paused and looked back at him. "I would never do that." I almost said I loved King, but I caught myself. "He's important to me."

Thatcher said nothing while he put the truck back in drive. Clearly, he was done talking. I wasn't going to say more either. I had to use this time while I had it.

I closed the door and headed toward the house. Thankfully, I was here before King returned, and I'd get to ask my questions. Hopefully, I'd also get some waffles and bacon. I wondered if she had whipped cream and chocolate sauce for the waffles.

• EIGHTEEN •

It's the only way I'm going to survive this.

RUMOR

Maeme took the seat across from me in the sunroom. "All right then, what do you want to talk about?" she asked, looking concerned, although I had assured her that the baby and I were fine. At least as far as I knew, we were. My lack of knowledge on this topic was why I was here.

"I threw up this morning," I told her. "I know that's to be expected, but I guess I didn't think about the fact that I know absolutely nothing about being pregnant. I mean, I ran a hot shower, and at the last minute, I realized it might be bad for the baby, so I cooled it down. What things are bad? Does second-hand smoke affect it? And what do I tell King when I get sick around him?"

Maeme reached over and squeezed my hand. "Breathe. It's okay. You're getting worked up, and there ain't no need. Women have been doing this since the beginning of time." She sat back and gave me a reassuring smile. "Now, there are a lot of rules and suggestions for healthy pregnancies that were not around back in my day. I'll get on the internet and order you a book. One that you can read, and it can give you direction. I want you and the baby to be healthy too. I can even get Doc over here this weekend to talk to you. He can answer all your questions, and we can see about getting you something for the nausea."

I nodded, feeling somewhat relieved.

"As for King seeing you sick, then I guess it was a blessing that he had to run to his house last night. I'll see what I can do to make sure he's not in bed when you wake up the next two mornings, and then by the time he gets back, Doc can have you all fixed up."

I let out a breath and relaxed for the first time since I'd thrown up. "Thank you."

She frowned. "Don't thank me. I take care of mine. It's what family does, and you are and will forever be family now. You're gonna be the momma of my great-grandchild. Speaking of which, are you hungry? Have you eaten anything?"

Hearing her call me her family put an instant lump in my throat. I didn't want to hold on to that too deeply. I wasn't sure what would happen once King knew. But I couldn't imagine Maeme would turn her back on me.

I fought back the tears and shook my head. "I came straight here."

She slapped the top of her thighs, then stood up. "Well, what sounds good to you?"

"Waffles ... and bacon," I said hesitantly.

She laughed as her smile spread across her face. "Then, waffles and bacon it is," she said, holding out her hand for me to take. "Come on with me to the kitchen. I'll get you some juice."

I took her hand even though I didn't need help standing up. I realized she needed me to take her hand more than I did. Once I was standing, she let it go and nodded her head toward the kitchen.

"RUMOR!" King's voice called out.

Maeme winked at me. "Right on time." Then, she cupped her hands over her mouth and shouted, "We're in the sunroom!" When she glanced back at me, she patted my arm. "He sounds worked up because you weren't where he'd left you. That's a good thing."

I wanted to believe her. Loving King and my need for him seemed to morph into something even more powerful now that I knew I had our child growing inside of me. I felt ... clingy. Having him with me soothed me. It gave me reassurance that he was always going to be there. That even though I was holding a secret that would change his life as he knew it, he would want me. Want us. The fear that it would push me away, however, was there, keeping me from letting myself hope for more. Believe that he'd one day love me too.

King stalked through the doorway, his gaze swinging to meet mine. "Are you okay?" he asked, concern furrowing his brow.

I nodded. I was now. He was here.

"Yes. I just came to see Maeme," I told him.

"And I'm making waffles. It's your lucky day," she informed him.

His eyes barely glanced in her direction before coming back to me. "Then, something is wrong," he stated, his eyes now narrowing as he took three long strides until he was in front of me. Cupping the side of my face, he studied me closely. "What is it?"

"Oh, for heaven's sake! I have company, and I want to make waffles. Stop acting ridiculous," Maeme said, but my eyes were on him. Soaking him in.

I almost pressed my cheek into his hand, aching for his touch. His security.

"I'm sorry I am just now getting back," he said, his eyes dropping to my lips. "I wanted to be with you."

"It's okay," I breathed.

He was here now. I had him with me.

"I'll go start breakfast," Maeme said, but King didn't look back at her or even acknowledge her words.

I wanted to thank her as she walked away, but with him looking at me like I was his breakfast, I found myself so mesmerized that I couldn't say anything. I was lost in King. His touch. His gaze. Being with him.

"I didn't like coming back to my room and you not being in my bed," he said as he ran his thumb over my mouth. "I fucking hate that you got in a truck with Thatcher."

I let out a soft sigh. "He just gave me a ride."

King shook his head, then lowered his head until his lips brushed the corner of mine. "Don't care. I hate it. I should have been there. You need something, and I take care of it."

I was a puddle on the floor—or at least it felt like it. I was on the verge of weeping—again—and throwing myself into his arms and begging him not to go this weekend, which I knew he had no control over.

"You're here now," I said before his mouth covered mine.

I slid my hands up his arms, wanting to pull him closer. A low groan vibrated his chest, and every nerve in my body responded. Shivering in response, I savored his taste. The powerfulness of how he wrapped his arms around me, pulling me closer to him until our bodies were pressed against each other, eased all the worries fighting for the number one spot in my head. He was here. This was enough.

"After waffles, we are going back to the stables," he said against my lips, then began to kiss a path down my neck. "I've got to stay buried in you until I leave. It's the only way I'm going to survive this."

I arched my neck, giving him better access. "We still have two days."

He paused, and although it was brief, it brought me out of the haze he'd been putting me under. The warmth of his breath heated my neck, and normally, that would cause me to tremble and sink further into the moment. But I felt it. The change in him. There was nothing good coming from that.

"I have to leave in the morning," he said gruffly.

I stilled. An ache already forming in my chest at the idea of him being gone.

"Why?" I asked, trying not to sound as pathetic as I felt.

More days with her. Alone. The two of them pretending.

"Orders. They want her out of town," he explained, his tone tight.

My hands slid to his chest, and I found myself grabbing handfuls of his shirt, as if I had the power to hold him. Keep him from going with just my strength alone.

"I hate this," he ground out.

"Me too," I managed to say, although the tightness currently squeezing my neck like a vise made it hard to say anything.

"Fuck," he growled as his arms completely wrapped around me and held me against his chest.

He buried his face in my hair, and I held on to him just as fiercely. We stood there in silence as the smell of waffles wafted into the room. I wasn't hungry anymore. Nothing sounded appealing. Not when I was faced with King leaving me.

· NINETEEN ·

I think you just ruined me.

RUMOR

"Maeme sent breakfast," King said, dropping off the food she had sent with us back to the stables.

Thatcher was the only one in the lounge room. He was sitting on the sofa, looking at his phone, but the mention of Maeme's food snapped his head up. "Smells like waffles."

"Because it is," King replied.

"Fuck yeah," he said, shooting up from his seat. His eyes swung to me, and he gave me a crooked grin that didn't fit him at all. "If she's gonna cook for you like this while you're staying there, then you just got a breakfast buddy."

King was tense as he turned, putting his body between the two of us, as if Thatcher was going to come close to me.

"Relax," Thatcher drawled. "I'm not the one with a hard-on for her. Sebastian's the one you have to watch, and he won't be here."

I slipped my hand into King's, trying to ease the tension rolling off him in waves. His much larger hand engulfed mine as he clenched mine tightly, and then he turned toward the door, taking me with him. His pace was fast and purposeful. As if he had to get me to safety and quickly.

The jealous, possessive way he reacted to others was the reassurance that I needed. I didn't complain. Knowing he wanted to keep me as his was exactly the thing my current emotional state clung to.

Shoving his bedroom door open, he nudged me inside, then slammed the door behind him. "Strip," he demanded.

I spun around, looking at him as he tugged his shirt over his head and tossed it away to land somewhere on the floor. The feral gleam in his eye was like a jolt of electricity between my legs. Reaching for the hem of my own top, I found myself mesmerized by his hands at the zipper on his jeans.

"Now, sweets. I'll rip that pretty little top right down the middle if I touch you."

My eyes widened as the image of his words played out in my head. A part of me wanted him to do just that. If I didn't like this shirt so much, I would let him. Reluctantly, I slipped it off. His eyes were on my bra with a hunger glowing in his gaze.

He made quick work of his jeans and boxer briefs, getting them off at the same time. My mouth watered at the sight of him, and I was so caught up in taking him all in that I forgot that I was supposed to be doing the same.

King stalked toward me then. "Not fast enough," he growled as he took the front of my bra, ignoring the clasp and jerking it open with one hard pull.

I heard the rip and gasped as his hands went to my shorts. My hands covered his before he could ruin them too.

"I got it," I said, quickly unbuttoning them, then shoving them down, shaking my hips slightly to get them to shimmy down my legs. When I stepped out of my bottoms, I used my toes to nudge them away.

King's hands clenched my hips tightly before he got my panties off by ripping them at the seams. Staring at the shredded satin fabric as it fell to the floor, I shivered. My feet left the floor as King picked me up and deposited me on the dresser.

"Open," he ordered, taking my ankles and putting my feet up on the smooth wood, leaving me exposed to him completely. "Fuck," he groaned before his head was there.

The first flick of his tongue sent a pulse of pleasure through me so hard that I cried out, burying my fingers into his hair, wanting to hold him there. It was more intense. Something was different. This had been incredible when he'd done it before, but it was better. My body. I was more sensitive.

"Goddamn, sweets, you taste fucking delicious," he swore as he began to go at me as if I were his favorite candy.

I was lost in the little jolts of nirvanic bursts. Letting go of his head, I had to lean back on my hands to keep from falling against the wall. This was more … almost too much.

It came on so fast and powerful that the world seemed to explode without warning. Screaming out his name, I lifted my hips to meet his mouth, trying to keep his mouth there as the crashing waves of sheer bliss shook me. While my body reeled from the power of my orgasm, I could hear King, but he felt far away.

"FUCK!" The roar that tore from his chest was matched with the hard thrust as he shoved inside of me. The sharp bite of his fingers dug into my flesh as he held on to my hips while he began to pump into me.

As I gasped for breath, my eyes flew open and locked with his. There was a primitive flare in his blue eyes. His jaw was clenched tight as he began to pound into me. The dresser thumped loudly as it hit the wall.

"Mine," he said through clenched teeth. "Mine," he repeated.

I lifted my legs, then pressed my knees against his ribs as the building promise of my climax drew closer. I was going to have another one. Watching his beautiful body flexed, damp with sweat, his veins standing out, as those eyes I loved looked at me like I was all he would ever need or want sent me breaking into another shattering orgasm.

"FU-UCK!" he shouted as he slammed into me one more time, then stilled. His body shuddering as his release began to fill me.

His arms wrapped around me, pulling me against his chest as he continued to pulse inside my walls, causing them to contract and squeeze. I shivered against him.

This was different. Sex with King had always been fantastic, but everything had felt elevated. There wasn't anywhere on my body not humming with pure pleasure. I clung to him as tremors still ran through me.

He ran a hand over my head, then wrapped my hair around his hand and held it tightly. "Jesus, sweets. That was … incredible," he breathed. He moved to press his lips to my temple. "I think you just ruined me."

Unable to keep from smiling, I turned my face to press against him as I listened to his heart beating rapidly inside his chest. It wasn't just me then; he'd felt it too.

What had that been? Why had it been so … so mind-blowing? I had no words to describe it.

We stayed like that, with him still inside of me, for several more moments while we waited for our breathing to level out. When he finally moved back enough to slide out of me, I wanted to sink my nails into him and hold him there. Keep him with me. This brought me a peace unlike anything else.

"Wait," I begged, not ready for this to end.

"You know I want to see it," he replied in a husky voice.

Shivering with pleasure, I watched him stand back, taking my legs and holding them open as his complete focus was there, where he had been. The dark, pleased look that came over his face made my heart clench tightly. It was kinky and possibly very twisted, but I liked it as much as he did.

He slid his finger over the tender entrance, and I sucked in air. His eyes moved to meet mine, and a devilish smile played over his face. "Nothing prettier than this pussy leaking my cum."

I sucked in a breath as my skin heated. He lifted the finger he had just slid inside of me. It glistened as he studied it. As if on impulse, my lips opened, and the animalistic expression that came over his face as he took his finger to slip it into my mouth made me feel as crazed as he was.

Closing my lips around his finger, I sucked hard.

"Jesus," he muttered in awe.

I used my tongue to lavish him with it as if it were his shaft inside my mouth.

He hissed as he slowly pulled it away. "All right, sweets, if you're gonna get naughty, then you're gonna get fucked again."

Licking my lips, I smiled sweetly up at him. "Promise?" I asked.

A deep chuckle came from his chest before he picked me up. I wrapped my legs around his waist just as his mouth covered mine.

· T W E N T Y ·

Of course he is. I don't shoot to maim.

R U M O R

The tenderness between my legs was all I had left of King for now. He was gone until Monday. I had to go five days without him. Maeme's library had gotten me through the afternoon after he drove away. The tears came even though I fought them, but at least I had been able to wait until he was gone.

Leaving the sofa in Maeme's living room, where I had been reading, curled up with a blanket that she had covered me up with, to go get a glass of water, I listened for any other sounds in the house. Maeme had gone up to get dressed for bed a little while ago, but she hadn't said good night yet. I knew I should try and get some sleep, but I was afraid that once I stopped reading, all the fears about King and Scotlin in Kentucky would start taunting me.

A loud ringing went through the house as I walked through the foyer. Pausing, I looked around. What was that? Had I caused it? The sound got louder, and I moved slightly to see if I'd triggered some alarm.

"Go to the back," Maeme demanded.

Turning, I saw her walking down the stairs with a hard look on her face I'd never seen before.

"What's wrong?" I asked as panic slowly began to unfurl in my chest.

Her eyes were locked on the door, then quickly swung to the front windows. "Get away from the windows!" she barked at me.

Scratch that. I was now scared. No, make that panicked.

I moved, but I didn't leave. I waited on Maeme. I wasn't going without her. If there was danger outside, I had to protect her. She wasn't just King's grandmother; she was my family too.

"Rumor! Go!"

I shook my head. "Not without you."

With a firm set of her mouth, she studied me for only a moment, then waved a hand toward the stairs. "Get in the closet under there."

I shook my head again. "Not without you," I repeated. "Do I need to call the police?"

The expression that flashed across her face looked as if I had just asked her if she'd like a piece of pie. "Lord, no. That ain't gonna do no good. Don't call anyone. Just get under them stairs."

"I'm not—" I started, but she cut me off, waving her hand as she swung her gaze to the door as the bell rang.

"Shit," she whispered, moving toward the door. "Stay there. Do not move," she said quietly before she lifted her other hand, and I saw it then. A gun. She'd had it the entire time, but I hadn't been looking at her side.

There was a click as she aimed it at the door with one hand, then used her other to open it.

As I stepped back, my eyes widened. What was she doing?

"Can I help you?" she asked in a hard tone that made me shiver and wrap my arms around my waist.

"Yes, ma'am," a deep voice replied. "I hope so."

"Better make it quick. I don't want to be stuck cleaning up blood off my porch."

The gunshot that went off wasn't from Maeme. It was farther away.

"Fuck," the man said.

"Not quick enough," she drawled. "Seems one of my boys is already here."

"I'm just looking for someone," he said, no longer sounding friendly.

"Only person here is me. Now, you can go before that one out there decides to aim at you instead of just giving you a warning. He's not what we consider sane."

I couldn't move. I was glued to the spot. Unsure of what was happening, but no longer worried about Maeme, who clearly had it under control.

"You got two goddamn seconds to get off that porch." Thatcher's voice carried in the house from outside.

I sank against the wall beside me then, letting out a sigh of relief. Although Maeme had a gun, the fact that Thatcher was outside made me feel a million times better. The man at the door should run like hell.

Maeme stepped outside, closing the door behind her. What was she doing? She wasn't needed out there. I moved toward the window, trying to make sure she was okay.

By the time I made it to the window, all I could see was Thatcher walking away with his gun pressed against the man's head. Searching for Maeme, I found her on the top porch step with her gun still aimed as her gaze scanned the yard. I sucked in a breath as the sound of a gun went off. Maeme's shoulders moved with the sound, and her arms barely jerked. A dark figure in the distance dropped to the ground.

"Get that out of my yard," she shouted before she turned and came back toward the door.

Stunned, I stood there as she stepped inside, scowling.

Her eyes found me the moment she closed the door, then narrowed. "I told you to get away from that window. They're bulletproof, but there ain't no need to test it."

I opened my mouth and closed it, then turned back to the window, staring out at the body in the yard. "Is … is … he dead?" I asked in a whisper.

"Of course he is. I don't shoot to maim," she replied. "Now, get away from the window, and let's go get you a cup of warm tea, then get you to bed."

"Bed?" I asked, my head still spinning.

"I reckon it's past both our bedtimes," she replied. "How's chamomile sound to you? Or did you like that peppermint tea I made you earlier?"

Tea? She was asking me about tea? There was a dead man outside in her yard that she'd killed. And Thatcher had another one with him that might be dead by now. I blinked several times.

"Come now," she replied. "They knew better than to come here. It's what happens."

"What happens?" I asked, stunned. "But … he … was asking about … he could have been lost. Or … " I couldn't seem to make my words come out clearly.

"An innocent man wouldn't have had a partner out, hiding in the trees. Ain't no through traffic back here. Folks don't come up to our doors—this door—asking for someone this time of night. They know better. Now, what kind of tea would you like? I think I might even have some raspberry."

My hand went to my stomach then. I laid my palm flat against it. Maeme's eyes dropped to see me do it. A small smile touched her lips, and then she looked at me.

"We protect what's ours. One day, you'll understand." She walked over to me and hooked her arm with mine. "I think this might call for some of my lemon cake too. You had a bit of a shock, but it was bound to happen eventually. Ain't no secret what we are now, Rumor. You know. It's our life. It's your life."

My life. My baby's life. I sucked in a breath as I fell into step beside Maeme as she headed toward the kitchen. I wasn't going to be able to eat anything. I didn't tell her that though. My heart was still in my throat. I wanted King. I hated him being gone. My phone was in the living room, and I glanced back in that direction, wanting to go get it and call him. Hear his voice. Be reminded why I was here.

An hour later, I was in bed alone. I sent a text to King and waited for a response, but one never came.

• TWENTY-ONE •

I didn't want to hear him lie to me.

RUMOR

The ringing of the phone woke me, and I reached for it, squinting against the sunshine pouring into the room. King's name on the screen had me scrambling to sit up as I pressed the phone to my ear.

"Hello?" I said, my voice thick with sleep.

"Hey, sweets. Did I wake you?" he asked.

"Yes, but it's fine," I replied, already smiling.

"You slept late. Did you have a hard time sleeping last night?" The genuine concern in his tone didn't seem as if he knew about what had happened here.

"Uh, I did. I just stayed up late, I guess," I said, not sure if there was a reason he didn't know about the men who had come here. Wouldn't Thatcher have told him even if Maeme didn't?

"I miss you," he told me. "I needed to hear your voice before I faced the shit today."

My hand held on to the phone tightly. "I miss you too."

"One night down. Only five more, and I'll be back."

"Yeah," I agreed, although it seemed like forever. "What are your plans today?" I asked, not sure I truly wanted to know, but suddenly afraid I'd say something I wasn't supposed to.

"Nothing important," he grumbled. "Shit I don't want to do. But hearing your voice helps."

My smile returned. "You can call me anytime. It's not like I have a busy schedule."

He was silent for a moment. "You bored, sweets?"

I twisted the sheet in my hand. "No, I'm fine. I have books."

"When I get back, I'm taking you riding. It's time you got to do more things."

The book Maeme had gotten me hadn't come yet, but I didn't need it to tell me that riding a horse was not safe while pregnant. Especially learning to ride one.

"The reading is fine. I'll go out for a walk today."

"Don't go alone," he urged.

I was sure walking back on Maeme's property or over at the Shephard Ranch was fine, but I agreed anyway. No need to make him worry. He had enough to deal with right now.

"We're gonna be late," Scotlin called out, causing me to tense up.

Were they in the same room?

"I'm sorry, sweets," he said with a sigh. "I gotta go."

I wanted to ask him if they were in a hotel room together. Where were they going? All the questions he wasn't voluntarily telling me made me fear I already knew the answers.

"Okay," I said.

"Talk soon," he replied.

I sat there, holding the phone as he ended the call, closing my eyes and taking several breaths, wishing it didn't hurt so bad. The words *I love you* had been right there on the tip of my tongue. Ready to fall right out if he hadn't hung up.

Dropping the phone to my lap, I covered my face and let out a deep breath, then forced myself to stand up. It was after ten, and Maeme had been up for hours at this point. I was surprised I had slept this late. The wave of nausea that came over me had me paus-ing, and I let it ease up before I continued onto the bathroom.

I glared at the toothbrush as I walked by it. Although it was a necessary item, I feared that using it would send me to the toilet again. Luckily, I made it through getting dressed and cleaning my teeth carefully without vomiting. The nausea was there, but it was manageable.

The house was bright and cheery, as always, when I walked down the stairs. My eyes went to the windows, and I thought about the man who had been killed out there last night.

Was there blood on the ground? Would the police come? What about the people who would be looking for the men?

I was lost in my own thoughts as I walked into the kitchen. Storm was sitting at the bar with a plate of food in front of him. His gaze shifted from his phone to me. "Morning," he said, setting his phone down and reaching for the mug beside him.

"Good morning," I replied. "You're not going to Kentucky?"

He shook his head. "Nope. Not this year. I'm here with Thatch and Wells."

I glanced at the coffeepot, then decided I'd better stick to juice and went over to the fridge.

"Maeme left you a plate of food," he told me.

Turning back to him, I frowned. "Where is Maeme?"

"She had to tend to some business," he said. "She'll be back shortly."

I took out the orange juice, then closed the door before going to get myself a glass.

"You seem to be handling last night well," he said.

I shrugged, not sure that was the case. When I turned back with my glass and filled it, I looked back at Storm. "What happened to that other man? The one Thatcher took."

"Dead. He told us what we needed to know, and then Thatch slit his throat."

I stared down at my orange juice as that sank in. He had said it as if it were no big deal. This would never be normal for me. How could I? That was someone's life they had ended.

"I spoke to King this morning. He called, but … but I don't think he knew about it. Last night."

Storm raised an eyebrow. "You think he'd stay away if he knew? Fucker has a death wish where you're concerned. He talked back to the boss as if his life was of no concern when it came to you. He'd tell them all to go fuck themselves and come running back here. Can't tell him. At least if you want him to live."

Blaise Hughes's face flashed in my mind. He'd been terrifying. Beautiful but clearly powerful and ruthless. I didn't want to think about King upsetting that man. My stomach knotted up.

"I see," I said because I did. I saw very clearly. We had to keep King there, doing what he was told.

I took a sip of orange juice and set my glass back on the counter.

"Did you know any of your hus—Churchill's friends? Business associates?" Storm asked me.

I shrugged. "Not really. I met some. He took me to parties, business affairs, that kind of thing in the beginning. I met people he worked with, but I didn't really know them."

Talking about Hill made me remember things that I wanted to forget. King made it easy to do that. He wasn't here now though.

"When was the last time you went to one of those things? Saw those people?" Storm asked me.

I tensed. It felt as if he was digging for something, and I didn't know what it was. I had nothing I was keeping from them. They knew more about Churchill than I did.

I shifted my feet uncomfortably. "About four months, I guess. Maybe three."

It had been hard for him to take me places because of the bruises I had to cover up. The last event where they took their spouses, I was limping and couldn't walk in heels. He was furious about it, too, even if he was the one who had hurt me. I'd paid for being injured with more abuse.

Storm pointed toward the oven. "Your food is in there, covered in foil."

I started to make my way over to it.

"You were three when you went into the foster system." It wasn't a question. It was a statement.

I nodded. I knew they already had my background. They'd known it before they went after Hill. Before I met them.

"Do you remember anything before then? Your mom? It says you had a mother, but doesn't mention your father. He's not even listed on your birth certificate."

I opened the oven and took out the plate that was warm. I didn't feel comfortable with this line of questioning. What was it that Storm was wanting to know? Why was I getting questioned all of a sudden?

"I don't know. My memories are vague," I said, closing the door to the oven, then turning back around. "Why are you asking?"

Storm was taking a drink of his coffee. He swallowed and studied me as if he was deciding if I was telling the truth. "There're a lot of holes. Things we don't know about you."

I tensed. "Join the club. There are things I don't know about me too."

Stone's lips twitched with an almost smile. "Fair enough. Sorry if I upset you. I'm just curious."

I took off the foil from my plate, feeling my hands tremble. "I think I'll take this to the sunroom. If you'll excuse me," I replied tightly as I grabbed a fork and walked away from him before he asked me more. About things I didn't know and had stopped trying to find out a long time ago.

It felt as if he didn't believe me. Like he thought I was hiding something. It was the first time I'd felt like a real outsider here.

I was ready for Maeme to get back. I didn't like Storm. I decided I liked him less than Thatcher. At least Thatcher was blunt. Said what he was thinking even if it was harsh.

The next two days, I only received one text from King. It was to apologize for not having time to call, and he'd sent it after I went to bed. When I responded the next morning, it went unanswered, although I could see that he'd read it. That stung, and my imagination was starting to get more creative and painful as the time passed. The more he went without contacting me, the more I seemed to get nauseated. I didn't know if it was because of the pregnancy or my own fear of him leaving me. Being done with me. Ready to move on.

Sitting at Maeme's, I was letting my imagination run away from me. Nothing was working as a good enough distraction. So, when Sebastian returned early from Kentucky and came to Maeme's to get me for a Derby party they were having at his house, I decided to go. Anything to get me out of my own head. My emotions were on overload.

I'd come to the conclusion I was sensitive because of my hormones. Storm hadn't meant anything by his questioning. He was right. There were gaps in my past that I couldn't fill in. I had once wanted to so badly. I'd even dreamed that I had a dad out there who wanted me. He'd come for me after finding out I existed and take me home with him. Give me a family. That fantasy had long since died though. It was one from my childhood. Like the one where he would swoop in and rescue me. Beat up the bad men who had been hurting me. In the end, I dealt with it myself. At least I had gotten away.

"I'm glad you came," Sebastian said to me as we walked toward the elevator doors in his underground garage.

"Thanks for getting me out," I replied.

I'd needed it more than he realized.

Knowing he'd been with King, I wanted to ask how he was, but I didn't. That would be admitting he hadn't called me but once.

"This is a small gathering. If I let too many of this bunch into the main house, Dad would be livid. The ones here are all cleared by security."

I nodded, stepping into the elevator beside him. "Today is the actual race, correct?" I asked, knowing very little about the Kentucky Derby.

"Yeah. We have a horse in every race. If not us, then other branches of the family. The Hughes—Blaise, he has the one who is running in the actual Kentucky Derby race. We all have some racing against each other in the other races. No one in the States has a horse that can beat Blaise's this year. There is no point in even trying."

I didn't care about Blaise Hughes, but I listened because this was King's life. I wanted to understand all of it. This was important to him and the family. He had never taken the time to explain any of it, and I wondered if that was because he saw me as temporary. My throat burned as I swallowed. That thought didn't sit well.

"We've got a bartender working tonight. You're gonna need to try one of the mint juleps," he told me as the doors opened back up and we stepped out onto a floor I hadn't been to.

I shook my head. "I don't feel like drinking anything with alcohol. Water is fine," I replied, hoping he would let that go.

He looked disappointed. "You sure? The females are all raving about them."

I nodded. "Yes."

"Go order one if you change your mind or just let me know."

"I will," I assured him.

The noise was slightly muffled by the two heavy wooden doors ahead of us, but not by much. Laughter and cheering filtered through. It sounded like a lot of people, not a small gathering. Sebastian stepped in front of me and opened the door on the left, then stepped back, waving a hand for me to go inside.

The chandelier that hung from the ceiling of the massive room made me think that this was normally a ballroom. Although right now, there was a wall covered in a screen with the happenings at the Derby displayed on it. Sofas, cushy chairs, a full bar, and tables full of food sat to the right of the space, and an ice sculpture of a racehorse sat in the center of it all.

There was so much to take in, and I felt as if I needed a moment. When my gaze landed on a topless woman who had on a wide-brimmed hot-pink hat, I sucked in a breath.

Sebastian moved up beside me. "I probably should have mentioned that. Clothing optional."

I didn't move. Was he joking? I swung my eyes back to him in shock.

He grinned and lifted an eyebrow. "Does that really surprise you?"

I nodded slowly. Yes, it did. This wasn't the lounge room in the stables. It was a … a ballroom they had transformed into something else.

"I, uh, I'm not taking off my shirt or any clothing."

His smile grew. "Thank fuck. We'd all end up with a bullet in us if you did."

He placed a hand on my lower back in the exact spot King always touched. I almost recoiled and had to force myself not to react rudely. He didn't mean anything by it.

"Storm and Thatch are here. So is Wells. After the other night, Dad wanted all of us here that could be, so he sent me home," he explained. "You saw how well Maeme handles things, but it doesn't mean that Ronan wants her to. Well, any of them really. They much prefer that she not have to get her hands dirty."

Did King know now? He hadn't called and talked to me about it. Was that even something he thought he needed to discuss with me? No, I was doing it again. I was letting my insecurities get the best of me. King was being kept from what had happened to protect him. He'd come back if he knew, and right now, Scotlin was his job. Not me.

A guy with pale blond hair that hung straight to his shoulders took a beer from the bar, then turned, his eyes locking on me, and he smiled. The way he held himself told me he thought more about his appearance than he should. He was attractive enough, but he was maybe five foot ten, and his brown eyes weren't anything special. They seemed to lack something.

"Come on," Sebastian said, leaning closer to me. "I'll get you a water." Then, he pointed toward the elaborate spread of food. "If you're hungry, help yourself. The lobster and shrimp were fresh caught and flown in this morning."

I nodded but followed behind him, unable not to watch as the topless woman with the pink hat grabbed a fancy glass from the table full of shrimp that looked like it had already been peeled. She stuck one in her mouth, then turned around to strut back over to where Thatcher was sitting with another topless female on his lap. Was he with both of them?

"I wondered where you had run off to," the blond guy said, drawing my gaze from the woman back to him. "You always did have excellent taste."

Sebastian shook his head. "Not mine. But off-limits," he informed him, then looked at me. "Rumor, this is Oriel. He is one of our newest trainers down at the stables. He's also a friend of Wells from his college days."

The blond guy leaned against the bar, smiling appreciatively at me. "It's nice to meet you, Rumor."

I smiled, not sure what I was supposed to say or even if I should say anything.

"She's King's," Sebastian said firmly.

This didn't seem to affect Oriel.

He shrugged. "I'm just being friendly."

"Keep it that way," Sebastian said, then shifted his attention to the bartender. "Water and my scotch."

"Or! Where's my drink?" Wells called out from the sofa.

"I'm being beckoned," Oriel said with a shake of his head and a smile that was meant to hide the annoyance, but I didn't miss it.

As he walked off, carrying a glass of whiskey that he had taken from the bar, a glass of ice water was placed in front of me.

Sebastian slid it over. "There you go."

I took it, then turned to see the screen while he waited for his drink. There was a sea of colorful hats as the camera scanned the crowd. Some people were talking about the upcoming race, but it was hard to hear over the noise in the room. I was just lifting the glass to my mouth when Scotlin's face appeared with a floppy white hat over her perfectly styled hair. She was laughing, and I could hear her name being said just as she tilted her head back. That was when I saw him.

King. Beside her. Looking down at her with a smile.

She was so close that his hand had to be around her back. Like he did with me. My breath caught in my chest as I watched the next three seconds that they showed him. The room went up in a roar at his image on-screen, but it all seemed so far away. There was a whooshing in my ears. When the horses replaced them on the screen, I was still unable to move. I sucked in air. My lungs had started to burn.

"She's just a job," Sebastian said near my ear.

I nodded, wanting to act like I believed that. But she'd been so close to him. They'd looked happy. Like they fit. Two beautiful people in a world that I didn't belong in. I swallowed hard and fought off the urge to run. At least no one was aware of my reaction. Just Sebastian. The others were drinking, enjoying themselves. I wasn't their concern.

Could I do this? Setting my glass back down before I dropped it, I clasped my hands in front of me so that Sebastian didn't see them trembling. Falling apart right now was unacceptable. I had to act fine. Convince Sebastian I was okay too.

"Rumor," he said, leaning down close to me, "he wants you. I swear."

I nodded, but couldn't force a smile. Not when my chest wanted to crack open. The sight of them was going to haunt me. He hadn't called me but once. Seeing him with her … I wasn't stupid.

I turned my head so that I could look into Sebastian's eyes. Read his answer even if he didn't tell it to me. "Are they sharing a hotel room?" I asked him.

There it was. The barest flicker in his irises that told me the truth.

"Never mind," I replied. "Forget I asked."

I didn't want to hear him lie to me. I'd had enough lies. I didn't want to know I'd been told another one.

"He isn't sharing a bed with her. That I can fucking swear to you."

No, he couldn't. No one could. No one knew what happened behind the closed door. She was stunning. Absolutely beautiful. He was a man used to getting what he wanted and when. He liked things I had never given him, and now, I couldn't. It would be dangerous to our child.

Closing my eyes, I inhaled deeply. I could survive this. I had to.

· TWENTY-TWO ·

You weren't supposed to fucking shoot him.

KING

The Derby had always been a good time. The energy, excitement, thrill of the win. I'd grown up loving it. Yet right now, I fucking hated every minute. Standing here with my hand on Scotlin's back while she continued to flirt and cling to me. I had to smile. Pretend I enjoyed it. Wanted this. I deserved a goddamn Emmy for this performance.

I just had to get through this party. Pretend like I was celebrating our wins today. Manage another night in that fucking suite that smelled like the overpowering scent of Scotlin's expensive perfume. Then, I was moving into another room and surviving one more day here.

"I'm getting a drink," I said, dropping my hand from hers.

She turned to place her hand on my chest. "Oh, would you get me a mint julep?"

"Of course," I replied, holding my smile. Hoping it looked like one a man gave his fiancée instead of the disgust that I actually felt.

Part of me had started to believe she had set this all up. Made up her own stalker or paid someone to do it. Just to force this. It was ludicrous, but I wanted out, and if I could prove something like that, I'd be free of her.

Getting distance from her, I took long strides toward the bar, needing to get away. Fresh air. Needing … fuck, I needed to bury my face in Rumor's hair and inhale. Run my nose along the soft skin of her neck and soak in the sweetness. Reaching into my pocket, I pulled out my phone to see if she'd responded to my last text. Still nothing. I'd sent her four texts and called every time I got a chance today. Maeme had assured me she was fine, not to worry. But I was about to call her again and make her put Rumor on the phone.

Why was she ignoring me? Had they put some shit on TV about me and Scotlin and Rumor had seen it?

My hand tightened on the phone as my head began to pound. This was bothering her. I hated it. I despised it. That hatred and fury were hard not to take out on Scotlin, especially when the world was watching. Just thinking about Rumor being hurt, I wanted to throw Scotlin away from me, demand she stop touching me.

"What can I get you?" the female bartender asked, leaning forward with a bright smile.

I wanted to roll my eyes.

"Maker's and a julep," I replied, looking back down at my phone.

I'd text her one more time. Check on things. Make sure she was okay. Just see her response. Know she was fine. I'd be back soon. Just one more day. Whatever was upsetting her, I'd fix it.

Texting out the words, I reread them twice, then hit Send. Just as I lifted my head, I felt it. The warning. The shift in the room. Something was off. My eyes scanned the room, then went to the entrances. The gunshot was followed by the sound of glass shattering, then screaming. Frantic people dropped to the ground, yells, shouts, then running.

My gun was drawn as I stepped around the man who had taken his date to the floor with him, blocking my path. There were seven other men in the room with a gun pointed. None of them the shooter though. They were all assessing, like I was. Gage Presley's eyes met mine across the room, and the trademark smirk on his face was gone. The deadly gleam I'd seen more than once was there now. He nodded his head to the left, and I turned to see Levi Shephard covering Scotlin with his gun also drawn. The shattered glass was directly behind where I had left her.

Fuck. Had that been for her?

Huck Kingston stood in front of Blaise, and both men had their guns drawn. Ransom Carver, one of the members of the Mississippi branch, glared angrily as he scanned the room with both his Glocks drawn.

Wilder filled the door, shoving past the people who were rushing from the room. His eyes scanned the area, then locked on me. He held it a moment, and there was a grim look that unsettled me.

What was that look for? Not because Scotlin was shot at. She was alive. They had either been a poor shot or a warning. What was it Wilder knew?

I moved toward him, stepping over people as security began to pour into the room. Lot of good they were.

Wilder shook his head as I approached him. As if I was going in the wrong direction.

"Scotlin," was all he said when I reached him.

"She's fine," I replied.

"The glass cut her. She's bleeding, and Blaise is watching you. Get over there," he said under his breath.

"What do you know?" I asked him, annoyed.

The stricken look in his eyes made my stomach sink and my chest tighten.

"Get to her before you get your ass shot for disobedience."

"Tell me," I urged.

"I can't. I'm being watched. Just get over there," he hissed angrily.

Annoyed, I walked over to Scotlin, who was hysterically clinging to Levi, who looked uncomfortable and like he'd rather be anywhere else.

Join the fucking club.

When she saw me, she let go of him and threw herself at me. Small cuts were on her arms from the glass, and several trickles of blood ran down them.

"OH MY GOD!" she wailed, clinging to me. "Someone shot at me."

"They missed," I said, pointing out the obvious.

Levi raised his eyebrows at me, and he looked like he wanted to laugh, but his lips didn't even twitch.

"Get me out of here," she begged, holding on to me as if her legs had been injured.

The people around us were all being led out by the security team, and the noise of voices, crying, and general hysterics got louder by the second. I'd happily like to get her out of here, then get on a plane south.

"This way," Levi said to me, then began moving toward the far-right exit, where Huck now stood.

Blaise was no longer in sight, and neither was Gage. We were all leaving out a specific door for a reason. There would be more of us there too. This was an attack on someone we were protecting. They'd gotten that close to her in a room full of us, which meant they weren't a poor shot. It was a warning. One for us. All of us.

Huck grabbed my arm as I started to pass him. I looked at him, narrowing my eyes. He wasn't the boss. He had about five fucking seconds to let go of me.

"Go on in," he told Scotlin with a nod of his head, leaving no room for argument.

She looked at me, not letting go. I decided I didn't mind him grabbing me any longer.

"You're safe. Go," I told her, pulling my arm free of her hold.

Thankfully, Huck's presence made her nervous enough to listen and obey. When she was gone, I jerked my arm free of his hold.

"What is it?" I asked him, preparing myself for more shit from Blaise that was going to piss me off.

"Your orders are to protect Scotlin," he said.

Tensing, I clenched my teeth. "I was getting her a goddamn drink. This room was full of family."

Huck cocked an eyebrow. "We know. That's not what this reminder is for."

Confused, I stood there, waiting for an explanation. "Then, what is it for, Huck? I'm here." Not in Georgia, where I wanted to be.

"It's a reminder to stay by her side."

"Did I say I was gonna leave?" I shot back.

He glanced over my shoulder, toward the door where Wilder was. I turned to see Wilder there, still looking like he wanted nothing to do with this. His expression was pained. I'd grown up with him. I knew him better than I knew anyone.

"What is it?" I demanded angrily. I was doing all I had been told to do even though I hated every goddamn moment.

Wilder sighed heavily and winced. He literally winced as he walked in this direction. Sliding his gun back into his holster at his hip. The closer he got, the heavier the weight on my chest seemed to grow. I didn't know what it was he knew, but I could feel it as if it were a physical thing.

"You have two minutes," Huck said, then turned and left through the door behind us.

My hands were fisted at my sides as I tried to calm the monster clawing inside me. Trying to take over. It wanted to break something. There was an unhinged craziness just under my skin. I'd never experienced this before, and I didn't know how to contain it. What had triggered it.

Wilder stopped, his eyes locked on me.

"WHAT?" I shouted, unable to contain the rage building.

"It's Rumor," he said.

Her name seemed to be the trigger that my inner beast had been listening for. It roared to life as I reached for my best friend and grabbed his shirt.

"What about Rumor?" I seethed, seeing literal red as I stared at him.

"She's missing."

The boulder that slammed into my chest took my breath.

No. I shook my head, dropping the hold I had on him, sucking in air. "NO!"

"Two minutes are up," Gage Presley drawled behind me.

I spun around, ready to take on everyone who stood in my way with my bare hands until I found her. She wasn't gone.

His gun was pointed at me. "She isn't your job. You only know because Wilder fought your case. That you should be told. Boss wants you with Scotlin. Go take care of her."

"LIKE FUCK," I roared, turning to stalk in the opposite direction.

I had to find her. How was she gone? Who could have gotten to her? I hadn't been there. I should have fucking been there! Goddamn Blaise fucking Hughes!

The sound of the gun was muffled with a silencer just before the sharp burn of stabbing pain tore through me.

"Goddammit, Gage!" Huck's voice shouted behind me.

I hissed, trying to manage the pain as my vision blurred.

"You weren't supposed to fucking shoot him."

· TWENTY-THREE ·

That normally only happens when the Mafia takes someone.

RUMOR

Sebastian was enjoying the celebration inside, and I hated to tell him I'd had all of tonight I could take. The cameras loved Scotlin May, and I'd been forced to see her with King so many times that I felt like my heart was slowly shattering. I knew King had said this was a job, and I kept telling myself that, but it was hard to watch nonetheless.

In the back of my head, I was being tortured with the thought that he could fall for her. He would see how good they looked together. They belonged together. Sure, they had a scarred past, but they'd been kids. What if the woman she had become was someone he could love? If he was going to fall in love with me, wouldn't he have by now?

I didn't want this baby—our baby—to be a shackle for him. I wanted him to choose me because he loved me. I'd already been married to a man who didn't love me. I knew how horribly wrong that could go. As much as I loved King, I wasn't willing to do it again.

Closing my eyes, I tried to block out the images of them together and just breathe. The evening air was cool, but I didn't mind it. Perhaps it could chill the fears running through my head. Giving me some kind of relief from it all.

It didn't help. Nothing was making this easier. Not even being outside. Peace and quiet might not have been the answer after all. I wasn't sure there was an answer. When King returned Monday, I'd know. I would be able to see it in his face. If he was done with me, then I'd be able to tell.

But how would I survive it?

The cloth that covered my mouth startled me, and it took me a second to react. Strong arms wrapped around my body as I shook my head, the little his hold allowed me to. I struggled to get air, shaking my head and trying to scream.

"Easy," a familiar voice said near my ear. "I don't want to hurt you."

I blinked, continuing to fight as panic began to build inside me. What was he doing? Did he want to smother me? Why? He just met me. I had barely spoken to him inside. My body started to feel heavy, and I struggled as things got slower, and darkness began to sink in around me. I was being taken under.

My arms fell limply at my sides, and I heard him whisper, "It's all gonna be okay," before the world went black.

A sharp, thudding pain in my head greeted me as I blinked, then closed my eyes again. My mouth felt as if I'd eaten cotton, and swallowing was almost impossible. I gagged slightly, then moaned from the ache it'd caused behind my eyes.

What was wrong with me? Was I sick? I needed to call out for Maeme. This wasn't right. The baby … would my being sick hurt the baby?

Maeme would never hear me like this. The house was too big. She would be downstairs. I had to get up. Even if it seemed as if movement might possibly kill me at the moment. Slowly, I opened my eyes again, hoping my phone was in sight. I could call her. Talking would be hard until I had some water.

God, why was my mouth so dry?

I stared straight ahead at a wall I didn't recognize. I hadn't been in all of the bedrooms in Maeme's house, but she would never put black-and-gold wallpaper on her walls, no matter how expensive it might look.

Where was I?

I tried to swallow again, and I couldn't manage it. The lamp on the bedside table was made of glass with golden patterns etched in it. Again, not Maeme's style.

This was bad, I thought. Or was it? Where had I gone to sleep?

Wincing, I forced myself to sit up and look around the room.

I tried to think. Remember what had happened last night. Pressing my temples, I pushed past the pain in my head. Had I drunk too much? My hand flew to my stomach. No. I hadn't drunk anything. I couldn't.

Had someone given me something? Had I been sick?

The races. The pink hat on the topless girl. Thatcher ... Thatcher bending her over a sofa and screwing her right there in front of everyone. The Derby. We'd watched it. King.

I closed my eyes tightly, gasping from a new pain. The one in my chest. King. He had been on the screen with Scotlin. They'd been close. Touching.

A knock on the door startled me, and I looked at myself, realizing I was wearing the sundress I had worn to Sebastian's house. He'd come to pick me up at Maeme's. He'd said I looked beautiful. Maeme had agreed and told him not to keep me out late.

Another knock, and then the doorknob turned. I backed up, unsure as to who it was since I had no idea where I was. A tall man with olive skin, dark eyes, neatly brushed black hair, a strong jawline, tall and muscular build, and arms covered in tattoos where they were visible entered. Then, he smiled. Even white teeth.

"You're awake. Good," he said, and I realized he had a glass of ice water in his hand. "You'll need this, I imagine."

I dropped my eyes from his face to stare at the glass. When he held it out to me, I didn't move. I had no idea who this was.

The cloth over my mouth. Oriel's voice in my ear. He'd been the last thing I remembered.

This wasn't Oriel though. Had Oriel brought me here?

"Take it. Please. You need to drink water. The chloroform knocked you out for fourteen hours. Your mouth must be fucking dry."

Chloroform? My hand started to fly to my stomach, but I stopped it and fisted the covers instead. They couldn't know about the baby. I had to protect it.

"What do you want from me?" I asked, my voice scratchy.

He held out the water to me. "Drink the water. We will discuss that later."

I stared at it, wishing I could swallow and wanting to down the entire glass. "What's in it?" I asked.

He chuckled. "Nothing. I want you clear and ready to talk. It is ice and water."

"I need to use the bathroom," I said.

I would get water from the faucet. I wasn't drinking anything he gave me.

He walked over and set the water on the bedside table, then pointed across the room to a door that was closed. "Right through there. I laid out fresh clothing for you and all you need for a shower. Please, take your time. Get refreshed, and then we will talk about why you're here over brunch."

If he thought I was eating his food, he was insane. Talking was hard with my throat feeling like sandpaper. I stood without a word and headed to the bathroom, ready to lock myself inside and try to figure out what to do.

Pausing on my way, I turned to look back at him. "Where is my phone?" I asked, knowing it was pointless.

He wasn't going to hand that over.

"It was destroyed and left outside where you were taken."

That response didn't surprise me. He'd used chloroform to take me. This had been a well-planned-out kidnapping. One I'd made too easy for them. I should have asked Sebastian to take me back to Maeme's. Going outside alone had been stupid. Especially after the incident outside Maeme's the other night.

The lavish bathroom was as bold in color choices as the bedroom. Everything was gold and white in here though. I locked the door, although I was sure the man had a key. Then, I went directly to the sink to get several handfuls of water and drink until swallowing no longer hurt. When I was satisfied, I looked at my reflection in the mirror. I was pale with dark circles under my eyes. Other than that, there was no damage.

My gaze dropped to my stomach. I wasn't sure about the baby though. How would chloroform affect it?

Nausea began to roll over me. I walked over to turn on the large walk-in shower before stripping off my sundress and panties. I needed to wash this from me. All of it. Being touched by strange men. Sleeping in a bed I didn't know. While under the spray of water that came from the ceiling like a rain shower, I checked my body for marks, then reached between my legs for any sensitivity to show that I'd been raped. There was nothing there.

I let out a sigh of relief, then tilted my head back and closed my eyes.

This was bad. Very bad. I needed a plan, but I'd never been taken before. Abused by a man I was married to? Yes. I hadn't won that battle either. I'd been saved. Would King find me and save me this time? Could he? No one knew where I was, including myself.

Opening my eyes, I scanned the contents of the shower to find shampoo, conditioner, and body wash. Both the shampoo and conditioner were the exact same brands I had used when married to Hill. A coldness settled over me. I didn't touch it. Instead, I turned off the water and got out quickly. My fear was slowly turning into a panic.

Why was the special brand meant for curly hair like mine in here?

I dried while my heart raced in my chest, then looked over at the panties, black leggings, a sweatshirt, and some thick socks that were lying on the counter. I didn't want to wear the clothes they had provided, but they covered me up more than the sundress I had been wearing. The desire to be covered from head to toe won out, and I took the things left for me.

Once I was dressed, I took several breaths and tried to push the nausea back while I focused on what I was going to do next. I had no options, except to face the man and find out what he wanted. My eyes swung back to the shower, and I shivered, thinking about the shampoo and conditioner. Hill was dead. King had helped kill him. This wasn't him. This was something else.

The Insantos? Was that it? They'd found a way into the family through Oriel and taken me. As tiny as it was, there was a small thread of hope. If it was the Insantos, then King would know how to find me. Wouldn't he? Didn't they have that kind of power?

"Please, please, please," I whispered before saying a prayer.

The next wave of sickness I couldn't hold back, and I ran to the toilet to throw up very little. Mostly the water I had just drunk. After a few more dry-heaves, I wiped my mouth and stood back up. Going back to the sink, I rinsed my mouth out and slowly sipped some more water.

Running my fingers through my curls to attempt to control the mess it was, I took a deep breath, looked in the mirror, and calmed myself the best I could. I had to be strong. Get through this. Be smart. Protect the baby inside of me.

When I walked back into the bedroom, the man was sitting on the high-back velvet chair that sat in the corner. He looked up from the phone in his hand, and a pleased smile flashed on his face, as if I had done something right. I hadn't showered to please him or worn these clothes to make him happy.

"I hope you feel refreshed. Let's go on down to the dining room. The vomiting should cease now. Side effect of the chloroform."

At least he didn't think it was due to morning sickness. Leaving with him sounded like a bad idea, but I couldn't stay in this room forever. Getting out was the best chance I had at an escape. I needed to see what I was up against. So, I nodded and waited for him to walk to the door before I followed.

I did my best to take in every detail. Anything that could help me get away. The hallway was wide, and there were other doors, but they were closed. The wallpaper out here was as over the top as the bedroom was. Dragons, monsters, in an Asian tapestry pattern that had gold all throughout with reds and blues on a black background. The staircase wasn't wide and impressive, but I also felt as if I was being taken down a back set of stairs.

After heading down another hallway with yet more horrible wallpaper, we reached a large opening with a gothic-looking chandelier and red walls. In the room, there was the largest sofa I'd ever seen in a massive circular shape. It was a solid black velvet. The man didn't slow until we reached two wide red doors that blended in with the walls. He opened them both, then moved back for me to enter.

Stepping inside cautiously, I took in the long dining room table, double the size of Maeme's. There was food on fancy gold serving pieces all down the center of it. A tiered tray sat in the middle with fancy pastries and fresh fruit and warming trays with small fires underneath the food. The man at the end of the table stood up then, and I saw the resemblance to the one who had brought me here. He was a slightly older version, except he wore a dress shirt and slacks, unlike the other man who was in jeans and a polo-style shirt.

"Mrs. Millroe," he said in greeting.

Although he was smiling as if I were an invited guest, I could see the glint of evil in his eyes. There was a threat of unhinged damage in that sculpted face. I wanted to correct him. Hearing Hill's surname attached to me made me cringe inwardly, but I didn't want to tell him my name. I was sure he knew it, but I chose to remain silent.

"This way," the man behind me said, waving a hand toward the chairs closer to the other man.

I continued to follow him as I scanned the rest of the room, but we were alone. He stopped and pulled out a chair to the right of the other man.

"I know you have questions," he began as I sat down. "My name is Falcon Socorro, and I have no intentions of hurting you. I need information from you, Mrs. Millroe." He paused, then held his hand up to motion for someone.

I heard a door open and turned to see two men walking in, wearing matching black attire, carrying trays.

"Do you prefer coffee or tea?" he asked.

I glanced over at him, not sure if he would remain nice if I refused everything here. If I went along with this, I could get information. Keeping myself from being beaten or killed was my goal at the moment.

"Do you have juice?" I asked.

He nodded. "What is your preference?"

"Orange," I replied.

One of the men stepped forward with a pitcher and filled the empty glass by the plate in front of me.

I started to thank him, but stopped myself. I wasn't going to speak unless I had to. Attention to detail. That was what I needed to do. That, and get as much information out of this Falcon Socorro as possible.

When I shifted my gaze back to him, he picked up his cup of coffee, flashing a gaudy diamond ring on his hand.

"Please help yourself to whatever you would like to eat. I've already had my meal, but I want to be sure you are full and satisfied before we begin."

I licked my lips and tried to calm my nerves before I spoke. "I would prefer we talk now. Why am I here? What do you want from me?"

He set his cup back down, and the flash of displeasure in his expression wasn't missed. He didn't like his directions to be ignored. He was in charge and gave the orders. If this was the Insantos gang, then I was willing to bet this was their leader.

"Your husband," he began, "stole from me."

I already knew this. He'd stolen from a lot of people.

I nodded my head once. "Yes. I am aware he was a criminal."

Falcon raised his eyebrows. "Was?"

Crap. I was going to hold that piece of information until it needed to be shared.

I managed a shrug. "I haven't seen him since he was attacked in his house and I ran. I don't know if he is alive or dead."

He studied me, and for a moment, I wondered if he was a human lie detector. It felt like he was with the way his dark eyes stayed locked on me.

"Tell me, Mrs. Millroe, why did you run?"

Sharing as much truth as possible might be the way to stay alive here.

"He beat me. I left, hoping the gunshot killed him."

He narrowed his eyes. "He beat you? Do you know who shot him?"

I shook my head, wishing I were a better liar.

He chuckled then, but his eyes showed no humor. "That's a lie, isn't it? You've been living under the protection of the men who shot him. Surely, by now, you are aware of that."

Not good. He'd caught me in a lie.

"Yes, I am aware. But I don't see how this concerns anyone other than me."

Another smile that felt as threatening as a snarl would have.

"I've not had issues with the family. They keep to their business, and I, mine. However, your husband owes me millions, and no one steals from me. I want my money, and I want his head on my wall as a trophy. You are the only person that I haven't spoken to who's connected to him. King Salazar made it difficult to get near you, so I had to wait it out and plan. Test their boundaries and priorities. Seems you are not one of those anymore with the future governor's daughter on his arm. I saw my opening and took it," he explained. "I want my money. What do you know about your husband's whereabouts? Any other hideouts he could be at?"

If I lied and he found out, it was likely that I'd die. A very brutal death. My hopes that King would come for me had just taken a hit. Was there truth to what he had said? King had been protecting me, but slacked off? Had I missed that? What if he'd wanted me taken? No. He wouldn't do that. Even if he was bored with me, he wasn't cruel. He cared about me. That wasn't something he could fake. I knew he cared. He'd begged me not to leave him and go to Ocala. I would not let this man convince me I wasn't important to King anymore.

"Churchill is dead," I said, hoping this wasn't a mistake and I ended up dead before the sun set.

Falcon leaned back in his chair with a thoughtful look on his face. "I see. Not surprised. I was beginning to think this might be the case when my men could find no sign of him. That normally only happens when the Mafia takes someone. They disappear."

He cleared his throat, then held up his hand and did that small flick of his fingers to beckon someone.

"I still want my money," he informed me as one of the servers came to fill his cup of coffee. "If Millroe is dead, then they've got all his money. His house is on the market, and I assume that was also the family's doing. He owed them money as well, and per usual, they took it back, along with everything else, including the wife. They don't leave a stone unturned." There was a trace of respect in his tone, mixed with annoyance.

I remained silent with my hands clasped in my lap. Speaking when spoken to was a rule I would abide. No need to give him more information than needed. He ran his fingertip around the rim of his cup as he stared at it in thought.

When he finally lifted his gaze to meet mine, he gave me a small nod. "Very well. You will stay here. They wanted you bad enough to take you, which means someone finds you important. When they hand over my money with interest, then they can have you back. That is, if you want to go back there. I'm an equal opportunity kind of man. I can see your appeal, and I am happy to offer you a place here."

Oh heck no. I shook my head. "I want my own life," I said. "They are going to give me that when I am safe." *From you, before I ended up pregnant.*

Now, I wasn't sure what my future held.

"I see," he said.

We sat there in silence for a few moments, and then he cleared his throat and set his cup down. "Then, you'll stay here until I have my money. You can return to them. I do not want a war with the family. We've managed to survive this long without issue, and I don't want to waste men and resources on that battle. I've heard the young Hughes is now in control, and his reputation is far more threatening than his father's."

Falcon stood up. "But the longer they make me wait, then I will have to use you to speed things up. Pain will be involved. I'm sorry in advance. Let's hope you're as important to them as I think you are. I truly hate to hurt a pretty face."

He beamed a bright smile at me then. "Now, eat. The food is excellent, and if I do return you to the family, I'd like to show you were well taken care of."

I sat there as he walked past me.

When he walked out of the open double doors, he snapped, "Tabor, Join Mrs. Millroe as she has her meal."

The man who had come to retrieve me walked back inside, and he gave me a smile that didn't look calculating. I felt somewhat relieved to see him even if he was the enemy. He wasn't the one who had threatened me.

"That wasn't so bad," he said, walking over and taking the plate that sat in front of me. "I'll just give you some of everything. You can eat whatever you prefer."

I said nothing as he did just that, then placed the overflowing plate back in front of me before walking to the other side of the table and taking a plate to fill for himself.

"The pastries are made fresh by our pastry chef. He trained in France for five years. They're delicious," he told me before taking three different ones from the tiered tray.

"What will he do to me if they don't give him the money he wants?" I asked, needing to plan. Be prepared.

He glanced up at me, then looked back down at one of the trays that sat over a small flame. "He won't do anything. One of our men will."

That didn't answer anything.

"And that would be?"

With a sigh, he straightened back up from leaning over the table. "Beatings, to start. They'll be filmed, and the video will be sent to King Salazar to see what kind of reaction we get. Falcon doesn't want to hurt you. He wants our money. That is all. Once he gets it, you'll be free to go."

I was finding that too easy. If it was this easy, wouldn't Blaise have already given them the money? They had it. Maeme said that I was wealthy. Why not give them that money?

"I have money," I blurted out. "What if I have them give you mine?"

He sat down across from me. "We don't want your money. We want ours."

"But you'll beat me to get it."

He tilted his head to the side slightly with a sigh. "Do you not think you're important enough for them to retrieve?"

Yes. I thought so. Maeme would want me back. King would too. Even if he didn't love me, he cared about me. We were friends first. There was something he felt for me.

"I think ..." I said, then paused, unsure how much truth they should have. Telling them I didn't know if they would might have them speeding up the beating portion. I couldn't let them hit me. "They will want me."

That would buy me time.

He smirked. "I agree. If not, he's an idiot." Then, he held up a pastry and winked before taking a bite.

I looked down at the food in front of me, and my stomach rolled. There was no appetite. I was almost positive eating would send me running for the toilet. But then I also had someone else to think about. Someone who needed to be nourished. This was no longer about me. It never would be again.

I picked up my fork and cut off a small piece of a pastry with raspberries in some kind of cream decorating the top.

"Do they know where I am?" I asked him.

"They are about to know. Falcon wanted to speak with you before he made his next move."

King would save me. I had to believe that.

• TWENTY-FOUR •

This is fucking Gage's fault!

KING

"Sit down, goddammit!" my father shouted as I stood up from the bed.

I glared at him, reaching for the wall to steady myself. "I need crutches and my fucking gun," I snarled angrily.

The motherfucker had shot me. I was going to kill him. But first, I had to find Rumor. The tight grip in my chest was more painful than the wound in my leg. I could handle any physical pain, but the sheer agony that clenched me at the thought of Rumor being hurt, taken from me, how scared she was—FUCK!

"You just had a bullet removed. SIT DOWN!" my father demanded as he stalked from across the room toward me.

"I swear to God, if you touch me, I will lay you out," I warned him.

He paused, his eyes flickering in surprise.

"Get me crutches, and I want my goddamn Glock."

The bedroom door opened, and Stellan walked inside. He looked at me standing and shook his head, then turned to my father. "Blaise is here."

My dad nodded as I fisted my hands at my sides. This was his fault. She had been taken from me because he had put her safety on the back burner. I didn't give a fuck if he was the boss. The former boss, his father Garrett Hughes, would never have let this happen.

"Stop scowling," Stellan said pointedly at me. "You need to remember who the fuck you are and who you answer to."

"They took her," I said through clenched teeth.

He nodded once. "And we will find her. But that man"—he pointed at the door and spoke in a low voice—"is the boss. He won't just shoot you in the leg to make his point."

I couldn't die today. Not when Rumor needed me. I tried to calm the fury rolling through me as I nodded.

Stellan stepped over to the door and waited like the soldier he was. He'd been in charge of the Georgia branch, answering to Garrett and now Blaise, since he had been twenty-seven years old. This was a life we'd all been born into, but right now, I didn't give one flying fuck. I wanted Rumor in my arms. Tucked safely into my side. I'd never leave her again. They could all suck a dick. Scotlin wasn't my job any longer. I'd wait until I had Rumor back, and then I'd tell them. If he killed me, then fucking fine.

Blaise Hughes walked into the room alone. It was rare that Huck or Gage wasn't at his side. He said nothing to my father or Stellan. His gaze was on me the moment he entered the room. I bit my tongue to keep from saying something that would have him ending my life.

"Falcon has her," he said matter-of-factly.

"FUCK!" I roared, unable to keep my mouth shut.

I ran my hand through my hair and gripped a handful, pulling hard. I had to get this sheer terror consuming me under control. It was taking over. I wanted to storm out of here and go get her, but my motherfucking leg was making that impossible.

Blaise didn't flinch. "He wants the money that he says is his from the buildings Churchill sold of his. He's asking for more than the buildings were worth. Over a million dollars more, to be exact.

He knows we have that and thinks he can demand it of me and get it because he has Rumor. *No one* places demands on me."

No. No, he was not going to let her stay there. I'd tear the place down to get to her if I had to.

"You'll have to put a bullet in my head to stop me from going after her," I spat, not caring about his power or his fucking pride.

"KING!" The fear in my father's voice was clear. He was sure I'd die right here, and if I didn't manage to control myself, he'd be right.

Blaise, however, didn't seem at all affected by my outburst. He studied me for a moment, saying nothing. I knew the man could have his gun out and put a bullet between my eyes in the blink of an eye. I had to save Rumor, and I couldn't do it dead.

"If I hadn't spoken with Maeme moments before walking in this door, you would be. Dead on the floor, that is. But unlike my father, when he stood in my position, I have one weakness. My wife and son. So, I have one question for you. Do you love her?"

I stared at him. I knew the story. We all did. He'd been obsessed with the woman he eventually married years before she knew he existed. He protected her. Took care of her from a distance. And when the man she thought was her father and the brother that she'd grown up with tried to sell her without her knowledge, he had killed them both and taken her. I wouldn't consider what he felt for his wife love because it was much stronger than that emotion.

I didn't trust love. It came and went. People changed. Moved on. It faded.

The sheer anguish that was seeping through every pore of my body because Rumor had been taken from me wasn't love. It was stronger. It didn't fade. I had already accepted that what I felt for her wasn't going to end. I would always want her. Hear her laugh, feel her sweet touch as she reached out to me. All the shattered pieces of my soul from the darkness in my life, she had put them together. She saw the good in me. Something no one else had ever looked for. She had found it and accepted me for all that I was.

"She's claimed my goddamn soul."

There was a small hint of a smirk on his face at my description.

"I see," he replied. "Then, you should know that they've not just taken Rumor, but they've taken your child as well. Maeme informed me that Rumor is pregnant. This means they've taken not one, but two family members. It's no longer about money. They've just brought hell to their doorstep."

I stood, stunned, unable to speak as he turned to Stellan.

"Get the men ready. Thatcher has the location. Gage is headed that way now. We take them all out. If they stand in the way, they die," he informed him, then left the room as Stellan followed him.

My eyes locked with my father's. He looked as completely shook as I was.

"Jesus Christ, Maeme," he swore as he ran his hand over his face.

When had she found out? How long had she known? Fuck! Rumor was pregnant. Was she sick? I had to get to her. She needed me. She had to be so fucking scared. She would be terrified for the baby. I was fucking terrified for them both.

Mine. They'd taken what was *mine.*

"Why didn't she tell me?" I asked, not sure it was directed at my father or not.

I would have stayed with her. Taken care of her. I'd have fought to stay there.

"Maeme. This is her doing. She knew you wouldn't finish the job. This was her way of protecting you and Rumor ... and my grandchild."

I sucked in a deep breath. The sharp, stabbing pain in my chest was worse than the gunshot to my leg had been. I had to get to her.

"Get me crutches," I said through clenched teeth.

My dad shook his head. "No. You can't go. It's the fucking Insantos. You can't walk."

"I'M GOING TO GET WHAT IS MINE!"

My father took two steps in my direction with his finger pointed at me. "If you want to be alive for your child's birth, then you will use your fucking head! We will get her. This is all our fight now. You heard Blaise. He's taking this personal."

"She needs me! It should be me going to get her. This is fucking Gage's fault!"

Dad raised his brows. "You know better than to mouth off to that psycho. You're lucky it was your leg he went for."

I felt fucking helpless as the beast inside me paced back and forth, wanting to go get what belonged to me and kill everyone in my path.

• TWENTY-FIVE •

I will fight until the very end. I swear it.

RUMOR

The four walls of the windowless bedroom seemed to get smaller and creepier, the longer I sat in there. I'd memorized every corner of it. Looked for anything that I could use in an attempt to escape. But so far, I had nothing. The door to the room wasn't even locked. They were so sure of their security that they didn't worry about my walking around.

Perhaps I should go out and get an idea of my surroundings. Mentally map the place out. Part of me thought it was a good idea. But there was a larger part that feared what I would find. Or who. How many of them lived here? Heck, as far as I knew, there was a guard on the other side of my door.

I laid my head back on the headboard and closed my eyes.

Did King know I was gone now? He had to. Sebastian would have eventually looked for me last night. He would have found I was gone. Realized I wasn't at Maeme's. King would have been told then.

I glanced over at the clock on the wall. It was already four in the afternoon.

Would I get fed again? Not that I wanted to eat, but I knew I had to. I tried not to think about the beatings that Falcon had mentioned if they didn't give him the money. Could I get him to not hit me near my stomach? Maybe he had a heart … or not. I didn't know for sure.

He could have already hurt me, and he hadn't. Either he wasn't completely evil or he was just that scared of the family. I had a feeling it was the latter. He seemed to not want to fight them. This was his way of just getting them to pay him. Why hadn't they done that already?

If he would just tell them that I needed to talk to King. Or even Blaise. I would talk to him. Tell him just to give Falcon all the money they had put back for me. I didn't need it. I could get a job, support myself. King would help with the baby. I knew he would. He was a good man even if he didn't love me. Besides, even if he wasn't a dependable guy, Maeme would make him do his part.

I'd lived in wealth, and it had been a hell I never wanted to go back to. Money did not bring happiness. In my case, it had brought a nightmare. Churchill had made sure of it. Being self-sufficient and depending on no one but myself was the most secure I could ever be.

A knock at my door brought me out of my thoughts, and I sat up straight as Tabor walked into the room.

His gaze found mine, and he gave me a small smile. "You doing okay?"

I almost lied but decided to be honest. "No. I'm scared."

"I see. You think they won't agree to the money."

I shrugged. "I don't know. I've met the boss once. He doesn't seem … like someone you can demand something from."

Tabor smirked. "Yeah. I've heard stories."

I sighed. "You must be used to dealing with people like him. I mean, this is a gang. So, y'all do what? Smuggle drugs, distribute, what?"

A low chuckle, then, "Let's leave story time for a later date if you're still here. But regardless of who we are and what we do, no one wants to tangle with the Hughes and the family that covers the South. They're the oldest organized crime family south of the Mason–Dixon line. That brings a power no one else can compete with. At least, no one has yet."

Crime family. That wasn't something that fit the people I knew. It made me think of something else completely different from the family I had been living with. I knew who they were, but it just was hard to see them that way.

"They have priorities," I said, slowly wanting to feel him out and see how soon this could go bad for me. At least in the sense that I wouldn't be in this room, being left alone. "I can't promise you that I am one of them. In fact, I am almost positive that I'm not. I was a … an accident, I guess. They shot Hill, my husband, and I ran. They knew I was there and followed me. They didn't plan on taking me, but they did to help me. Y'all were not something they anticipated. They didn't know they were getting mixed up in more of Hill's shit."

Tabor shrugged. "Well, we will see. That's all I can tell you. My brother is a patient man if it means he will get what he wants. However, if his switch is flipped, he can be unreasonable. I don't know you, but after meeting you, I'd hate to see you be at the receiving end of it."

My gut twisted. This wasn't what I'd wanted to hear.

"Even if I can get him the money? I have it. I just have to get it."

Tabor shook his head. "No. He won't take your money. He wants what is his. My opinion is that taking on the family is a mistake. But a part of him thinks this is his chance to show dominance."

"So, he will beat and kill me, but not take my money?" I asked.

He nodded.

I dropped my head into my hands and sighed. How was I going to get out of this?

"Are you hungry?" he asked.

I shook my head, then stopped. Not about me. I still had to fight for my child. Lifting my head, I looked back at him. "Yes."

"I'll have a meal brought up to you. Any requests?"

He was taking my order as if I wasn't the prisoner and bait. "Whatever you have."

"Very well," he replied, turning and walking back out of the door before closing it with a soft click as he went.

Tears stung my eyes as I sat there in silence, feeling helpless. There had been no response from the family. Blaise hadn't offered the money yet. If he hadn't already, he wasn't going to. I'd be beaten, and the videos would be sent.

Would he react to that? Would King be able to do anything even if he wanted to?

Placing a hand on my stomach, I whispered, "I will fight until the very end. I swear it."

I had to do all I could for the baby inside me. Lying down and taking it like I had with Hill wasn't an option this time. This wasn't just me. I had someone to protect, and I was going to do everything I could to keep her safe.

Her. I didn't know if it was a girl or boy, but somehow, saying *her* just felt right.

· TWENTY-SIX ·

He'll kill everything that moves and not pause as he does it.

KING

"You realize we are both going to end up fucking shot," Wilder said, cutting his eyes at me in the passenger seat of the black Escalade he was driving.

"I've already been shot," I replied bitterly. "They can't expect me to stay in a goddamn hotel room in Louisville while they go after what is mine."

Wilder sighed heavily. "I know. I get it. Trust me, I've been there. It's why I broke you out when your dad said they were leaving you there until it was over."

Glaring at my phone, willing it to ring with an update, I muttered a string of curses. "Fucking Wells. I'm killing him first. Then, I'll find that goddamn Oriel."

"Easy," Wilder said. "Wells is being handled. He didn't know he was being set up. But, yes, he brought the bastard into our lives. Oriel, you can kill. Torture. Whatever makes your dark heart happy."

Slamming my hands on the dash, I let out an angry growl, wanting to kill someone. Anyone at this point. The building explosion happening inside my chest was going to kill everything in its path.

"They'll have her soon. Thatch and Gage are leading the pack. No one will be left standing or breathing."

"I SHOULD BE THERE! ME! She needs ME!"

Wilder said nothing. He knew I was right. If this were Oakley, he would be just as furious and out of control.

"What if this was Oak AND she was pregnant?"

He glanced at me with a solemn expression. "That's why I'm doing this. Like I said, I get it. I'd be just as messed up." He looked back at the road. "As for Gage, when Shiloh finds out he shot you because you were going after your woman, she'll tear him a new one."

I didn't know the women who belonged to the Ocala men, but if there was a woman who could handle Gage Presley, then she had to be fucking evil. Nothing like Rumor. My sweet, beautiful girl who didn't have a fierce bone in her body. She was too good for me. She deserved better, but I'd be damned if I was letting her go. I didn't think I'd ever planned on it from the moment she had climbed into my truck.

My phone started ringing, and my heart slammed against my chest frantically as I answered it.

"What?" I snapped.

"Where the fuck are you?" Stellan barked into the phone.

"Driving to your house from the airport." I left out that Wilder was the one who had come and gotten me.

"Fucking hell, King! Can you not do what you're told?"

"Not when my woman has been taken," I snarled. "What is the update? Who is going, and where do I meet them?"

"Stubborn ass," he muttered. "They're already gone. Thatcher, Gage, Huck, and Storm are going in with Blaise. Wells and Sebastian, along with three of the Ocala guys that came with Huck. Ten of the Mississippi boys and five from the Alabama branch are with them. It's an army. Led by lethal weapons. She's going to be brought back safely. You can't go in there like you are. It will be a hinderance."

"She needs me!" I argued, knowing he was right. I didn't need to be in the fucking way, but I'd be damned if she came out of there, thinking I didn't give a shit. No one else was going to hold her.

"Put it on speaker," he said.

I pressed the button. "It's on speaker."

"Wilder," Stellan said.

"Yes, sir."

"I'll send you the location on the burner phone. Take him there the moment I send the go-ahead. I'll make sure she is brought out to him directly. That's the best I can do, King. Anything else, and someone will be killed."

My jaw was clenched too tightly to respond. I just nodded my head once. Rage rolled inside of me because I knew I couldn't go in there and find her. That the first face she saw wasn't going to be mine. I fucking hated it!

"Got it. But, Stellan," he said, glancing at me, "he's on edge. Not gonna be able to hold him back long."

"I know. It won't take long now. Not with Blaise there. He'll kill everything that moves and not pause as he does it."

"Yeah, I know," Wilder replied, then ended the call.

"When the location comes in, go directly there. We aren't waiting," I told him.

"I never thought we were," he replied.

I stared straight ahead, trying to work through the throbbing in my head and the monster demanding I go and get what belonged to me.

· TWENTY-SEVEN ·

Fuck, I guess he gets to live.

RUMOR

I had taken the fork that had been brought with my meal and slid it underneath the blanket before putting my napkin haphazardly over my plate after I finished. When the maid came to take my plate, she didn't even notice the missing utensil. Sitting on the bed, I kept my hand wrapped around it, reminding myself I had something, that I wouldn't be helpless.

I considered hiding it and going in search of something more, maybe a knife, but I hadn't worked up the nerve just yet. The thought that I might do something that would make Falcon start beating me sooner kept me here.

There was a strange sound in the hallway, and I tensed. Had they realized I'd kept the fork? A loud thud startled me, and I shot up from the bed where I was sitting with the fork gripped tightly in my right hand. I started to run to the bathroom when the bedroom door swung open, and a man came stalking in with a bloody knife in his hand. I froze, staring at him in horror. There were two red sprays over his shirt that could only be blood.

"Rumor?" he asked with a cocked brow.

I glanced at the bathroom door again, knowing I couldn't get there in time. So, I held up my fork, which was ridiculous, considering he had a terrifying knife that he'd used recently on someone's vital arteries, if I had to guess.

The man's face was misleading. If he'd walked in here without being covered in blood and a knife, I'd have thought he'd come from a photo shoot. He didn't look like a man who sliced people open, but then what did I know?

His smirk as he looked at the fork in my hand didn't surprise me. It was rather pathetic.

"A fighter. That's good," he drawled. "If it makes you feel better, keep your fork, but I'll handle anyone who comes at us, yeah?" He nodded his head toward the door. "You ready to blow this joint?"

I lowered my hand. "Who are you?" I asked, afraid to be hopeful.

"The calvary. Let's go," he said, then turned and headed for the door.

I glanced back at the room and decided I was going with the crazy knife man. When I got to the door, there was a man lying on the ground with a slit in his neck and lifeless eyes staring at nothing as blood pooled on the floor around him.

I lifted my horrified gaze to the man who was responsible for it, and he grinned, then winked at me. Was this man insane? Perhaps I was making a mistake. He started down the hallway, and I jumped over the blood and hurried after him. Insane or not, he was clearly getting me out of here. I'd worry about who he was and why he was here to get me once I got out.

When we reached the stairs, there were two more dead men, and one was missing eyeballs. I covered my mouth to silence the scream I couldn't stop.

Oh God. Oh God. Where were his eyes? I was going to be sick.

"Don't look at it," the insane man I was following called back to me as he kicked the first dead man out of the way and continued down like this wasn't a living horror show.

I almost cried out in relief at the sight of Storm as he walked into the foyer.

He took in the dead men on the stairs and gave the man with me a disgusted look. "His eyes? Really?"

The man who I was following shrugged. "He pissed me off," he replied, then pulled something from his pocket and tossed two eyeballs into the air before catching them with a chuckle.

"Jesus, Gage," Storm muttered, then turned to me. "You okay?"

He knew the psychopath that I was with. Thank God!

I nodded, fighting back the emotion clogging my throat.

He walked over to me and held out a hand as I hurried down the stairs, passing the man he had called Gage. They had come for me. This was ... this was the family's doing. For me.

"Where's King?" I asked.

"He'd be here. That's on me. But I found you," Gage said behind me.

He wasn't here? My heart sank, and the burn in my eyes only got worse as a tear broke free and rolled down my face. Was he still with Scotlin?

My hand went to my stomach, and I tried to take a deep breath to calm down. I was okay. We were safe.

"Where are the others?" Gage asked.

"Blaise put a bullet in Falcon's head and chest. Huck broke Tabor's neck. The others that you didn't slice up have been taken down," Storm informed him. "I'm taking her with me."

Tabor was dead? They'd broken his neck? My stomach rolled, and I turned before bending over and throwing up the food I'd been fed earlier.

"Fuck," Storm said behind me as he took my hair and held it back. "Sorry about that. Too much information. My bad."

Several heaves later, I stood up and stared at him, still in shock. Was this really how they handled things?

Storm took the hem of his shirt and ripped it, then handed it to me. "Here. Wipe your mouth."

I did as told as he took my elbow.

"Time to go."

I went with him numbly through the house, not looking around as we went for fear of what I might see. I didn't think I could handle any more death. When he opened the door leading outside, I let out a small sob. I was leaving. I had survived this.

"RUMOR!"

I would know the deep voice that called my name, even in death.

My head snapped around as King moved toward me on crutches. I shoved past Storm and ran to him.

Why was he hurt? What had happened? I reached him, and he dropped both crutches as his arms wrapped around me.

He buried his face in my hair and inhaled deeply. "Fuuuck, sweets. I think I died ten goddamn deaths since I was told they took you."

The tears that I'd been fighting off broke free as I clung to him, sobbing. His arms tightened, pulling me to him.

"I got you," he murmured. "This will never happen again. I swear to God."

His scent eased me, and I nodded my head, not ready to speak just yet. He'd come for me. I meant something to him. He cared.

"Did they hurt you?" he asked, gently pressing a kiss to my head.

I shook mine. "No," I croaked out.

Although it didn't matter. They were both dead now. Along with several others.

"You good? I need to go help. Two of Linc's guys were shot. Gotta get them to Doc," Storm said behind me.

"Wilder will get us back. Thank you, Storm," he said fiercely.

"Don't thank me. Gage got her," he replied.

King's arms tightened. "Fuck, I guess he gets to live."

Storm laughed then. "*He* gets to live? Dude, you didn't see what his crazy ass did to the men in there. Forgive and forget, bro."

King pulled back enough so he could look at me. "You swear you're okay?"

I nodded.

His eyes dropped to my mouth, and he ran his thumb over it. Then, he looked back into my eyes. The possessive gleam made me shiver. Every small cell in my body hummed. I wanted that.

"And the baby?" he asked softly.

I gasped, speechless, staring up at him.

He knew. How did he know? Had Maeme changed her mind?

"I think she's fine. I need to see Dr. Drew. The chloroform …" I stopped explaining, hating to think it had hurt her.

His jaw clenched as he glared at the house behind me. "We will go straight to Maeme's and get you checked."

"You know?"

Was that why he had come? Because I was pregnant? Had Maeme told him so he would come get me? Had it taken that to make him care? All my fears and insecurities came rushing back.

"Yeah, sweets, I know," he replied, his expression softening.

He started to lower his mouth to mine, and I placed a hand on his chest and shook my head to stop him.

"I just threw up," I told him, covering my mouth, realizing my breath had to be horrid.

His brows drew together. "Pregnancy?" he asked.

"I saw some things."

A stricken expression came over his face. "Come on. Let's get you home."

He turned then, and I saw him wince. His leg. I'd forgotten. I wrapped my arms around him as if I could hold him up.

A small smile tugged at his lips. "My crutches."

I let him go, then bent down to get them both, handing them to him, hating seeing him like this. "How did you break your leg?" I asked as he walked with me back toward a black SUV with a man standing outside of it, leaning on the hood with his arms crossed over his chest, watching us.

"Shot. Not broken," he replied.

I stopped. "Shot?" I asked, horrified.

He paused and looked at me. "I'm fine, sweets. It'll heal faster than a damn break."

"Who shot you?"

He scowled then and glanced at the man who was no longer in front of the SUV, but opening the back door.

When King looked back at me, he sighed. "Gage."

I frowned. Why would Gage have shot him? Weren't they on the same team or whatever?

"Let's get in the Escalade," he said. "Cleanup is about to be here."

They had a cleanup crew for this kind of thing?

I followed him to the vehicle and let him get inside first wanting to help him if needed. Then I climbed inside closing the door behind us. The other man was now in the driver's seat.

He turned his head to look at me. "Nice to meet you, Rumor. I'm Wilder Jones."

I managed a smile even though I was still trying to wrap my head around the fact that Gage had shot him. "It's nice to meet you too," I replied.

"Come here," King said to me as he stretched his arm out on the back of the seat.

"Will I hurt you?" I asked, looking down at his leg.

"No, sweets," he assured me.

I scooted back, and his arm came around me to pull me so close that my head was resting on his chest. He kissed the top of it.

Wilder began to drive away as I lay there, letting the relief completely sink in. I was with King. We were both alive. I closed my eyes, inhaling his smell. This was where I always wanted to be.

"Why did Gage shoot you?" I asked as I traced patterns on his abs.

"Because he's a dickhead," King replied.

I decided not to push it. Maybe I didn't need to know.

• TWENTY-EIGHT •

Doesn't mean I have to like it.

RUMOR

Maeme was out of the door the moment we made it to the porch, throwing her arms around me.

The tight hold she had on me as she let out a, "Thank you, Jesus," left me with the urge to tear up and laugh at the same time.

I was positive Jesus had had nothing to do with my being here. There was nothing Christlike about the slit throats and trophy eyeballs that Gage had pulled from his pocket.

"Doc is downstairs, working on stitching up one of the boys from Mississippi and giving another one a blood transfusion, but he's already got the ultrasound machine set up and is waiting on us," she said, patting my arm as she pulled back and looked at me with watery eyes. "But you're here, and you are okay."

I turned back to King, who stood there with his crutches, and noticed the dark circles under his bloodshot eyes now that we stood under the light of the porch. He looked pale and weak.

Panicked, I let go of Maeme to turn to him. "You need to lie down. Get off your leg. Sleep," I told him, wrapping my arm around his waist.

He chuckled. "Sweets, I'm not lying down without you. And I sure as hell am not letting you go down there and have an ultrasound without me."

"But you look pale and like you might pass out," I argued.

"I'm fine. Stop worrying and get your sexy ass in that house."

"Come on now. We will see to both of you," Maeme said, opening the door and ushering us inside.

King was good with crutches, I realized. Really good. I had a feeling this wasn't the first time he'd ever used them. I walked beside him as we followed Maeme to the stairs leading to the basement.

Then, she paused and glanced at King. "Do you need the elevator?"

He shook his head. "I'm good."

Elevator? I hadn't known there was an elevator.

She didn't argue with him, but I wanted to demand he use this elevator. I turned to look back at him, and he grinned.

"I got this, sweets."

"What if you fall?"

He leaned close to me and pressed a kiss to my closed lips, which I was not opening until after I brushed my teeth.

"I've walked down these stairs in worse scenarios. Crutches are child's play."

"But there is an elevator. Why?"

He cupped my face. "Because it only fits one and I refuse to be away from you for a fucking second."

Oh. I stared at him, wishing my mouth didn't taste like vomit. I wanted to kiss him. Tell him I loved him. Instead, I turned and walked down the stairs slowly in case King needed me to catch him.

When we were both at the bottom, I sighed in relief.

Stellan, Ronan, Monte, Barrett, and Roland were all sitting in the sofas around the coffee table. They were looking at me and King.

"Good to see you, Rumor," Ronan said.

What did I say to that? Thank you?

"She's been through a lot. Not up for talking," King said, placing a hand on my back. "Come on, sweets."

None of them said anything more as we passed them. A man I didn't recognize stepped out of one of the rooms. He looked to be about King's father's age, but he wasn't dressed like the older men. His jeans, cowboy boots, and fitted black shirt reminded me of something King would wear. The tattoo that wrapped around his arm looked like chains.

When our eyes met, he looked familiar.

"Rumor, this is Linc Shephard. Stellan's brother. He runs the Mississippi branch of the family."

The eyes. That was it. He had Stellan's eyes. Although that was where the similarity ended.

"It's nice to meet you. I'm sorry you have hurt men because of me."

He shook his head. "Not your fault."

If I had stayed inside, like Sebastian had told me to, then it wouldn't have happened, but I didn't have time to argue. I wanted King to sit down. He looked like every step he took was painful.

Linc walked past us toward the room with the other men. Dr. Drew stepped out of the furthest room on the right, followed by Maeme. She was smiling.

"Come this way," she said.

Dr. Drew gave me a reassuring look as I passed him and stepped into the room.

King didn't allow more than a few inches of space between us. When he looked at the doctor with a scowl, I realized he was still angry about my checkup. Did he not want the doctor to do this? We needed to check the baby, and I liked Dr. Drew.

"Oh good Lord, King. He delivered you. He's stitched you up more times than can be counted. Stop acting like he wronged you," Maeme scolded him. "You've already choked him out over it. Let it go."

I spun around and gaped at King. "You did what?" I asked him, horrified.

He threw one more glare at the doctor before looking at me. "He touched what was mine."

"I am pregnant, King. He has to check me."

King flexed his neck and popped his jaw like he was trying to calm down. "Doesn't mean I have to like it."

"Ignore him," Maeme said. "Lie on the table, Rumor."

"I'll also need her to pull her bottoms down just above her pubic line. Can he handle that?" the doctor asked.

"YES," Maeme declared. "I will handle him. And if this doesn't work and you need to do an internal one, I will call Stellan and Ronan in here to deal with his crazy ass."

"Like hell!" King snapped at his grandmother.

She stepped around the table and jabbed his chest with her fingernail. "Do. Not. Speak. To. Me. Like. That. Again."

To my surprise, King actually simmered down somewhat. I looked between the two of them before climbing onto the table.

King moved past his grandmother to stand beside me, taking my hand in both of his. I lifted my eyes to look up at him. His perfect face was tense as he watched the doctor setting things up.

"You want to pull her pants down for me?" the doctor asked.

King moved then and gently tugged the front of my leggings down, keeping his hand lying flat over my pubic bone as if he was hiding something. If I wasn't so worried about him taking out the doctor, I would laugh at this behavior.

The doctor glanced at him, then looked at me. "Normally, the gel is cold, but Maeme made sure yours was warmed first," he said with a smile before he covered my stomach with the clear gel.

I turned my head to the screen as he began the ultrasound. I didn't know what I was seeing, but I held my breath as I waited until he said something.

A small thudding sound filled the room.

"That's the heartbeat," he said with a smile. "Nice and strong."

King's hand tightened on mine as I kept my eyes glued on the screen.

"This," Dr. Drew said, "is your baby."

I sucked in a sharp breath, barely making out the small pea shape growing inside of me.

"Measuring right on schedule," he added. "Everything looks just fine."

Turning to look up at King, I realized he was watching me. The awe in his expression took my breath away. He wanted us. Both of us. The words *I love you* were right there. I had to fight to keep from blurting them out right now.

The paddle on my stomach was removed, and King pulled up my leggings, covering me, then tugged my shirt into place. His need to keep me covered made me feel special. As if he saw me as something he cherished.

"Maeme tells me that you have a lot of questions and concerns. She's ordered you a book, but I have one, too, that I brought you. My cell number is on the front. Call me, text me, with any questions you have. It doesn't matter the time. Also, I brought you some pills to help with the nausea."

King helped me sit up while he balanced on his crutches. I reached for the book and took it, feeling as if I had just been given gold.

"Thank you," I breathed, clutching it tightly.

He gave me a quick smile, then stood up. "I need to go tend to my other patients. If you don't have any other questions for me, that is."

I shook my head, feeling guilty that there were people here who had been injured while saving me, and he was in here, giving me an ultrasound.

"Thank you. Please, go help them."

He glanced at King before turning and leaving.

Maeme's sniffle reminded me she was still there. I shifted my body to get off the table and looked over at her. She was wiping away tears and grinning.

"Oh my," she said with a laugh. "I didn't know I was gonna get so emotional."

Then, she came and gave me a quick hug before turning to King. She squeezed his arms and looked up into his eyes, saying nothing before leaving the room.

When I looked back at King, he was watching me. I wanted to know what he was thinking, if he was happy. Or did this make him feel trapped? I wished he'd say something. Let me have an idea of what he felt.

"Let's go to bed," he said.

I nodded, knowing he needed to lie down. All my worries could wait. Getting him healed was most important right now.

· TWENTY-NINE ·

I got shot for defying my boss, wanting to come find you,
and you should ride my dick like a good girl because of it.

RUMOR

When I opened my eyes, King's erection was pressed firmly against my bottom, and his arm was wrapped around me with his hand tucked between my legs. His thumb moved and rubbed directly over my clit, causing me to gasp.

A deep chuckle behind me told me he was awake and knew exactly what he was doing.

"Sit on my face, sweets."

I turned over to look at him. His eyes were no longer bloodshot, but hooded as he stared at me with a sexy grin on his face. I was also relieved to see the dark circles were gone from under them.

"You're hurt," I reminded him.

"Yeah, I am. And the only thing that will make me feel better is your pussy riding my tongue."

I felt my entire body flush, and I clenched my thighs together. "Don't you want breakfast?"

He bent his head, brushing his lips over mine. "The breakfast I want is between your pretty thighs."

Dear God, this man.

I returned his kiss, wanting nothing more than to do exactly what he wanted of me. But he had been shot, and he needed to rest. He didn't need me to be getting off with his mouth.

"But what you need is a good meal and rest," I replied against his mouth.

He groaned, then reached for me and pulled me over on top of him until I was straddling his body. "Sweets, there isn't a meal that compares to your cunt. That's as good as it gets."

I covered my face and laughed. He knew how to make me beet red and turned on, all at the same time. His hands grabbed my hips, and he moved me down until I felt his hard length press against me.

"If I can't get it on my mouth, then I want it on my dick," he said in a husky voice. "I'm hurt, sweets. The least you could do is ride me like your favorite horse."

I squirmed, causing him to groan and my entire body to hum with pleasure. "I don't have a favorite horse."

He grabbed the sides of my panties and ripped them, then tugged the fabric from my body. "You're about to have one."

"King, you're hurt," I started as he lifted his hips and shoved his boxers down until his cock was free.

"That's right. I got shot for defying my boss, wanting to come find you, and you should ride my dick like a good girl because of it."

I stopped the rocking my body was doing of its own will and stared down at him. "What?"

"Fuck me, sweets."

I shook my head. "That's not what I meant. You got shot because you defied Blaise?"

He grabbed the top of my thighs and pushed me back until the tip of his erection lined up with my entrance. "No one tells me I can't go get what's mine," he said. "Now, lift that perfect little ass up and let me sink into that needy pussy."

Unable to tell this man no even if I wanted to discuss this fur-ther, I did as he'd told me to. The moment I pressed down on him until he was fully seated inside me, he threw back his head and let out a deep, low sound in his chest. For a moment, I was lost in the sheer beauty that was the man beneath me. The way his tanned skin flexed, his muscles standing out. I could spend the rest of my life looking at him and never grow tired of it. The dark, heated look in his eyes when he opened them made me tremble with excitement.

"Ride me, sweets," he said just as his hand smacked firmly against my right butt cheek.

Leaning over him, I grabbed on to the headboard and lifted my hips, then dropped back down onto him.

He grabbed my ass with both hands and growled, "Fuck, that's it, baby. Such a good girl, taking my dick."

The moment the dirty talk started up, I knew I was gonna be done fast.

He leaned forward, grazing my nipple with his teeth. "Damn, those are the prettiest fucking tits I've ever seen. They're bigger."

I'd noticed that too. They were more sensitive as well. I bit my lip as I bounced on him. This felt different. My body was needier. It craved being filled. A frenzy was building in me, and I locked my eyes on King's face as I began to press down harder and faster.

"Ah! Ah!" I cried with each jolt of pleasure, wanting more. Panting, I dropped my hands to his shoulders and chased the orgasm that was coming. I had to have it.

"Fuuuck, sweets. You keep this up, and I won't be able to hold off," King said before spanking me harder than before. "My baby likes to ride after all."

"King," I moaned as the first tingle started to unravel.

"That's it. Come for me. Squirt all over my cock," he said, breathing heavily.

With those words, it slammed into me, causing my body to jerk several times as the gush of my release pulsed so hard that it ran down my thighs and his.

"FUUUCK! That's mine!" he shouted as his hips lifted and his body tensed up.

The warmth of his release shooting into me sent me off again, and I dropped down onto his chest, my face buried in his neck as I continued to have burst after burst of this complete euphoria.

When it finally began to ease, King's arms were wrapped around me, his cock buried inside me. I sucked in a breath and then exhaled slowly. My heart was still racing as I relished in the best sex of my life.

"Sweets, if this is what pregnant sex is, then you're gonna fucking stay knocked up for the rest of our lives."

I giggled, pressing my face into his collarbone. I had kind of gone a little wild. But wow. That had been incredible.

He trailed his fingertips down my back and over my bottom several times as our breathing slowed.

"I think I'm more sensitive," I said.

"No shit," he replied, causing me to laugh again.

"Is that bad?" I really hoped not.

"Depends."

I lifted my head to look at him. "What does that mean?"

He reached up and brushed the hair out of my face. "On if you like walking bowlegged. Because I'm about to fuck you again and possibly after that. I'm thinking I might keep you in here and fuck you for the next nine months."

I grinned, pressing my lips together.

"You like that, don't you?" he asked, taking my chin and pulling my mouth down to his. "Just think, I could have eaten your pussy, then fucked you. Next time I tell you to get on my face, you do it."

I wasn't going to argue. I sank into him, savoring the taste of him as he held me. No matter what the future held, I had this with him right now. If I lost him one day, I'd be devastated, but it could happen, and when he bored of me, I would hold on to these memories.

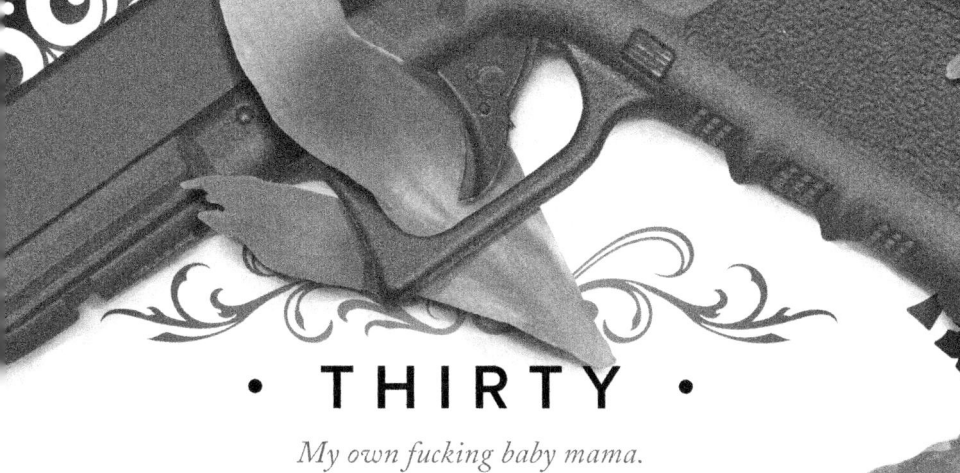

· THIRTY ·

My own fucking baby mama.

KING

I walked back into the bedroom to find Rumor standing there in nothing but a towel. Her head full of damp ringlets that I fucking loved. I was down to needing one crutch today, but it would be a week or more before I was free of the added support. Thanks to Gage fucking Presley.

"You're back," she said, smiling.

The way her eyes lit up when she saw me made my chest feel like it was gonna explode. Jesus, was there anything she did that I wasn't obsessed with?

"Meeting was short," I told her.

"Are you hurting?" she asked, concern shadowing her face.

Yeah, it hurt like a son of a bitch, but I wasn't telling her that.

"No, sweets. Can't feel a thing."

She didn't look convinced. "You need to rest. Sit down. I'll get you something to drink, and you can watch TV."

Damn, she was cute.

I let my gaze travel down her body slowly. "I'll sit if you come straddle me. Naked."

She shivered and held on to the towel tightly. "We just … had sex twice," she replied, but I could tell she wasn't against it.

"And you're naked in a towel with all those pretty curls wet and hanging down your back."

"Shouldn't we talk?" she asked softly.

My eyes shot back up to her face. "Talk?"

She nodded, those big eyes of hers looking at me nervously.

I took a step in her direction. Damn crutch made everything hard. "What do you want to talk about, sweets?"

She shrugged, and it was real hard not to drop my gaze back to her tits. They were at least a size bigger.

"The … baby."

I nodded. "Okay. Yeah, if you want to."

I watched as she pulled her bottom lip between her teeth, then let it go.

"Do you not want to?"

I wanted to do whatever the hell would put a smile back on her face. And possibly get her to either sit on my face or dick. Her choice. But clearly, she was worried about things, and I needed to reassure her.

I nodded toward the sofa. "Let's talk," I said. "But as much as this pains me to say, you need to put some clothes on. I won't be able to focus on much else if you're sitting there in a towel."

A small laugh escaped her, and it was like a fucking shot of heroin to my system. I loved that sound. I wanted to hear it all the time. She stepped into the closet to get dressed. Her modesty was cute. I'd seen every inch of her body, but she still couldn't get dressed in front of me. I didn't say anything to her about it because if she dropped that towel for me, I couldn't promise I wouldn't bend her over and pound that tight cunt again. Talk be damned.

I walked over to the sofa and dropped the crutch before sitting down, then propped up my injured leg. I rested my head against the wall and trained my eyes on the door of the closet. When Rumor walked back out, she was dressed in a pair of black shorts and a white tank top that was cropped enough so that when she lifted her arms any, the smooth, tanned skin of her still-flat stomach showed. I narrowed my eyes, not sure I was okay with her leaving the room like that. I didn't want anyone seeing her stomach. That was mine.

"Why are you frowning?" she asked as she walked over to sit next to me.

"Shirt is too short," I replied.

She looked down at it, then back at me. "Your aunt gave it to me."

"Don't care."

Rumor tilted her head to the side and smiled at me. I was pretty sure she could get away with anything when she smiled like that.

"King."

"Sweets," I responded, reaching for her hand and threading my fingers through hers. "Talk. I'm listening."

She took a deep breath, and that only made her tits bounce.

Fuck, concentrate. Not on her tits either.

"I didn't mean to get pregnant. I was taking the shot. I didn't lie to you to trap you," she said.

"I never thought you did."

Where was she going with this? I watched as she chewed her bottom lip so hard that I was about to save it before she hurt herself.

Thankfully, she let it go. "And you are okay with this? You don't feel trapped?"

Trapped? What the fuck did she mean?

I shook my head.

Her dainty shoulders lifted and fell.

Was she frustrated? What had I said wrong?

"King," she said, looking at me pointedly this time, "I want this baby. But that doesn't mean I intend to lock you into anything. I know this is a for-now thing, until we are … done. But with a baby, sometimes, it can feel like you are trapped. I want you to be a part of her life, but I am not demanding it. Or anything of you."

I couldn't sit here and listen to any more of this. "Stop."

Rumor closed her mouth, eyes wide as she looked at me.

I shifted so that I was facing her. "What the fuck are you trying to say? Because right now, it sounds like you're trying to tell me I'm not required in your life or our child's life. And I'm telling you right now, that shit ain't gonna fly."

She opened her mouth and closed it again. I was tempted to pin her to the sofa and fuck her into submission. Make her scream my name and tell me who she belonged to until I had her so damn full of my cum that it was running down her legs like a motherfucking waterfall.

"I don't want to trap you."

"You mentioned that," I pointed out.

She nodded and licked her lips. I wanted to lick those lips.

When she threw up her hands and stood up abruptly, I leaned back, ready for the rest of whatever this was she was trying to say.

"YOU are and will always be this baby's father," she said, placing a hand on her stomach. "But that doesn't mean we are a package deal. You can be the father and not be my … whatever … boyfriend?" She shook her head, looking frustrated. "I will not use our baby to control you. You can come and go as you please. When I'm not here anymore, that is, and we are somewhere else. The baby and me."

What the actual fuck?

I dropped my wounded leg to the ground and leaned forward. "You saying you're gonna leave me, sweets? Because I'll hunt you down. I'll tie you to my goddamn bed."

I stood, ignoring the crutch, and took a step toward her, feeling the urgency to tie her up now and not give her the chance to go anywhere. Fuck her until she realized she wanted me. She wanted to be here with me.

"I can make you want to stay," I warned her. "You start talking about leaving, and I'll never let you out of my sight again. What the fuck did I do that made you want to leave? Consider leaving? You think you're gonna get bored of me? Because I can rip those fucking shorts off right now and bury my face between your legs until you're begging me to never stop."

She blinked. "I don't want to leave."

"Then, why are we talking about it? You're clearly thinking about it!" I shouted, feeling the panic that she might actually want to leave me one day.

I couldn't lose her. She couldn't leave me.

"YOU!" she said, pointing at me. "You will get tired. You said this would end. That relationships didn't work. Love wasn't real."

I paused. Fucking hell. I had said all that. Before. All before I got so damn addicted and obsessed with her that I didn't realize I would never allow her to leave me.

"Love is weak," I said, taking another step toward her. "It fades."

She looked stricken.

Reaching up, I cupped her face in my hand. "So, it's a fucking good thing that you possess my soul, sweets. You're under my skin, in my blood, locked so damn deep inside of me that I could never let you go."

Her lips parted as she looked astonished.

Had she not already known this? What more could I have done to show her?

"This isn't about me being pregnant?" she asked softly. As if she was afraid to know.

Damn, I had failed at this already, and we were just getting started. She had no idea.

"I got shot before I knew you were pregnant. I told Blaise and the rest of the family to fuck themselves and turned to come find you, not having any idea you were carrying my baby. All I could think was, I had to get to you. I didn't give a damn about anything or anyone else. But you were gone, and YOU are mine. My reason for waking up in the mornings. So, no, sweets. This isn't about you being pregnant. But right now, I'd be lying if I said I'm not fucking relieved you're tied to me because, apparently, you're not as sure about the future as I am."

She closed the space between us, grabbing my face and pressing her soft lips to mine with so much force that I had to put weight on my bad leg to keep from falling backward. I wasn't gonna let her know that though. Not when she was kissing me like she couldn't get enough.

I held her, giving her back as good as she was giving and relishing the sweetness that was only Rumor. I'd called a lot of women sweets, but until her, none of them had really owned the title. She did. It was hers.

Moving my hands down to grab her ass, I squeezed, pushing her up until I had my hard dick rubbing against the crotch of her shorts.

"Makes me think you want to keep me," I said against her lips.

"Yes," she said breathlessly.

"That's my girl," I said, smiling as I took her mouth again.

She broke free and stepped back suddenly, confusing the fuck out of me.

"Your leg!" she squeaked. "I am so sorry! Sit down."

"I'm fine."

"SIT DOWN," she ordered, surprising me.

I backed up, grinning as she looked at me sternly. When I sank back onto the sofa, she moved to take my leg and prop it back up.

"You have to be more careful."

"I'll do whatever you want—on one condition."

She narrowed her eyes. "What?"

"Take off those clothes and sit in my lap for the rest of the day. I swear I won't get up again."

A laugh burst out of her. "Seriously?"

"Deadly," I assured her.

"Do you always think about sex?"

I nodded. "Yes. I think about fucking you every waking minute, sweets."

"You won't be thinking about it when my stomach is big and round."

I reached out and grabbed her hand, tugging her to me. "You'll have my kid growing inside of you. My own fucking baby mama. Yeah, I'll think it. I'll worship you like the goddamn queen you are."

The musical laughter that trickled out of her as she fell onto my lap made every damn thing that was wrong in my life right.

"King," she said softly.

"Yeah?"

"I love you, and it doesn't feel weak. It feels like the most powerful, real thing I've ever known."

· THIRTY-ONE ·

I'm just trying to keep the man from going feral on anyone.

RUMOR

One would assume a week of being fucked several times a day and treated like the sun rose and set at my feet would give me enough confidence to face the fake engagement party being held tonight. But it was with the man I loved. The father of my child pretending to be engaged to another woman. That was hard. Very, very hard. Perhaps if I didn't have all these pregnancy hormones racing through my body, I could focus. Be the support he needed to handle the job. Keeping it all in and not making this difficult for him was all I could do.

The knock on the door was a welcome interruption from the thoughts haunting me. I took one last look in the mirror. The dress that Annette had sent to me through Maeme was unlike anything I'd ever worn. The wedding dress that Hill had chosen for me was simple. He'd called it elegant, but I'd thought it was kind of plain. This was elegant. Not to mention expensive. The tag that had still been on it when I opened the hanging bag caused me to rub my eyes and squint to make sure I'd seen that correctly.

I picked up the silver clutch that Maeme had brought with the dress, but all that was inside of it was my phone and some lipstick. Then, I walked over to open the door to the bedroom I'd gotten ready in at Maeme's. It was no longer called the blue room. She referred to it as my room, and something about having a room that was considered mine warmed my heart. Sure, I missed the cottage, but I also didn't feel safe being alone. Even if the Insantos had been … wiped out.

Sebastian smiled at me, then let out a low whistle. "Damn, Rumor. He's gonna fucking kill me."

Yes. I was afraid of that too. Not because of how I was dressed, but because Maeme had insisted that I not go unattended to the engagement party. Of course she had waited to share this with me until after King left to go to the Kingstons' house to prepare for the party. They were setting up extra security and planning a course of action if the man who was stalking Scotlin decided to show up. Their hope was he would, and they'd be ready for him. King had told me last night that they believed he was someone on her father's political campaign.

"You sure you don't want to change?" Sebastian asked, rubbing the back of his neck.

I shrugged. "I have nothing else. Annette sent this dress for me to wear, and Maeme approved it."

He simply nodded and let out a nervous, clipped laugh. "Of course they did."

I waved a hand at him. "You look good in a tux."

A crooked grin curled his lips. "Thanks."

It was the truth. He was an attractive man, and I was sure he was well aware of it. Seeing him like this made me anxious about seeing King. He'd be dressed in one too. Remembering how he looked in a tux made my heart flutter. Scotlin would be clinging to him, and that was going to be painful, but I would be the one he came home to.

"You're ready then?" he asked.

"Yes. Might as well get this over with."

"My thoughts exactly."

He stood back so that I could lead the way. Maeme was standing at the bottom of the stairs as we descended, and a big, bright smile lit her face when she saw me. She was dressed in a pale blue satin dress that hung to the floor. Maeme was a beautiful woman, but seeing her like this had me awestruck.

"Good Lord, you are a sight. I knew that green would match your eyes. You are breathtaking."

I started to thank her when Sebastian spoke up.

"No shit. I thought you loved me, Maeme. King is gonna lose his shit when he sees her, and I'm the one he's gonna murder when he does."

Maeme rolled her eyes. "Don't be so dramatic. If she has to go watch King pretend to be engaged to Scotlin May, then she needs to feel confident, beautiful, and know she's the one he can't stop looking at."

"Tonight, he needs to be looking at Scotlin and be on alert in case the stalker is there."

Maeme shrugged. "He will do his job. Besides, there is so much security there that no one is going to be stupid enough to make a move."

"We need them to. This fake shit with Scotlin has to end soon. Especially with Rumor pregnant. King has become more unhinged. He can't keep this up."

Maeme nodded. "Yes, I know. I'm going to speak with Stellan about it."

"Oh, he fucking knows," Sebastian drawled behind me.

When I reached the bottom step, Maeme hugged me, then took my clutch. "I have something for you."

She put her hand into her pocket and pulled out a small wand-like thing.

"Maeme, seriously?" Sebastian said beside me.

I glanced up at him, seeing his brows drawn together. He didn't look like he agreed with whatever that was she'd put in there.

"I can't give her a gun yet. We gotta teach her how to handle one first."

"If someone gets close enough that she needs to use that, then King's gonna gut him anyway."

She shrugged, handing me my purse back, then patted my cheek. "It's a Taser. An illegal one. Very effective. It'll have a grown man three times your size on the ground in less than a second. Use it if needed. At any time you feel threatened or unsure about your safety, get it out and have it ready."

All I heard was *illegal*. She'd put something illegal in my purse.

"We should go. Don't want to be late," she said, turning for the door.

I followed her with Sebastian coming out last and locking up behind us. The limo that was parked in the driveway shouldn't have been surprising. A tall man with wide shoulders and an intimidating expression stood beside the vehicle. He opened the door as we approached, and Maeme said something to him that caused a small smile to tug at his lips before she climbed inside. I just hoped tonight went the way they all wanted it to and that I never had to use the illegal Taser in my purse.

The Kingstons' home was even more lovely at night, all lit up. I felt as if I had stepped back in time and was walking into a party among the elite in the deep South. Maeme turned to us as we approached the steps to the entrance.

"You're her date," she scolded Sebastian. "Give her your arm, for goodness' sake, boy."

Sebastian glanced down at me and smirked, then held out his arm for me to take. "I'm about to die, and she doesn't give a shit," he whispered, causing me to press my lips together to keep from laughing.

We stepped inside the house behind Maeme, and the man standing just inside, greeting people, I had never met in person, but I knew his face. All of Georgia knew his face. Jefferson May.

And his wife, Marigold, stood beside him. They were the solid, church-going Republican family of the South. There had never been a tarnish on their name. People adored them. I wondered what all the folks of Georgia would think if they knew he was connected to the Mafia.

"Maeme Salazar." Jefferson May beamed with a big smile on his face. "It's been too long."

Maeme stepped forward and shook his hand, agreeing, then hugged his wife, Marigold. When she stepped back, she held out a hand toward me and Sebastian. "You both know Sebastian," she said. "The lovely lady at his side is Rumor Beauregard. She's a close family friend." The way she said it made it very clear that I was important to her and the rest of the family.

Sebastian stepped forward and shook Jefferson's hand, but his smile looked less cheerful and more forced as he cut his eyes over to me. There was an odd expression in his perusal. As if he was studying me while trying not to be obvious. Was it because of King? Did he find me a threat to Scotlin? I hoped I was reading this incorrectly. When he shook my hand though, I could see a flicker of unease in his eyes. I wanted away from this man. My internal warning was on high alert, and when we turned to leave them, I took a deep breath, thankful that was over.

It could be that I had made that all up in my head, but I couldn't get past the way he'd stared at me, as if ... he knew me. And he didn't want to. My thoughts were so focused on the odd encounter that when we walked into the ballroom, I didn't immediately notice King standing beside Scotlin. Not until Sebastian's arm flexed underneath my hand as he tensed.

King was everything I had remembered in a tux and more. The flutters in my stomach at the sight of him caused me to suck in a breath. He was beautiful. When our eyes met, I wanted to see him smile. Have that reassurance that he was mine. But there was no smile. No secret exchange of affection. The glower on his face made it very clear he was angry. Perhaps *furious* was a better word.

"And here we go," Sebastian muttered.

I slipped my hand from his arm and took a small step toward Maeme, who was speaking to Scotlin. King's eyes held mine while his entire stance went rigid.

"King, dear, you need to smile. It's a party," Maeme said, squeezing his arm tightly, as if to warn him to behave. When he didn't even acknowledge her, she turned toward me, smiling as if all was well in the world. "Sebastian was kind enough to escort Rumor so she wouldn't be alone. Isn't the dress Annette sent perfect on her?"

King cut his eyes toward Sebastian, and the threat was there in his eyes for anyone who was looking to see.

"Honey," Scotlin cooed at him, touching his arm and leaning into him, "if you want a break from greeting people, we can take one. Just say the word."

He didn't budge or respond to her. His eyes shifted back to me. I smiled nervously, not sure what I was supposed to do now. He didn't want me here, but I hadn't asked to come. Maeme had insisted. Otherwise, I would be at home with guards I didn't know.

Right now, that option was looking like a much better idea than this. My eyes stung, and I knew it was silly, but I wasn't reacting well to the glare from King, directed at me. He never looked at me like that.

"Sebastian, why don't you take Rumor to meet some people and get her something to drink?" Maeme said with a happy tone, turning from King. She patted my arm as she walked past me with a swish of her long skirt, not saying anything more to King or Scotlin.

I dropped my gaze to the floor, wanting to find somewhere to hide and stay there.

"Of course," Sebastian replied, giving King one last look before touching my elbow.

"Don't." King's voice was so cold that it caused me to shiver. "Don't touch her."

Sebastian's hand dropped away from me immediately.

"Got it," he replied with a smile that didn't reach his eyes.

Then, he nodded at me to come with him. I didn't look back at King, but I could feel him. His eyes felt like a hot flame, following my every move.

When we reached the bar, Sebastian finally glanced down at me. "Water? Soda?"

"Water is fine," I replied.

"Still or sparkling?"

"Still."

He turned to the bartender. "Ice water and four shots of Maker's."

My eyes widened as I stared up at him.

He pulled at the collar of his shirt. "I'm gonna fucking need it," he explained.

"He's mad," I whispered.

"You think? We will be lucky if he doesn't murder someone tonight. Try not to look ... well, just ... if you can, don't be any more appealing than you are."

I frowned. "What does that mean?"

He sighed. "I don't fucking know. I'm just trying to keep the man from going feral on anyone."

"Is he mad at me?"

Sebastian shook his head. "No. He's fucking livid that you look like that and he can't stake a claim. I don't know what Maeme was thinking. She should have put you in a muumuu or some shit."

A small laugh escaped me, and he grinned briefly, then shut his expression down almost instantly.

"Don't make me smile at you. His ass will be on me in fucking seconds."

Unable to help myself, I glanced back at him, and his heated glare met mine. Scotlin was speaking to him, but he didn't look away from me. His eyes slowly traveled down my body, causing me to feel warm all over. When he reached my face again, I smiled softly, wanting to reassure him, but it didn't help. He didn't return my smile.

"That's enough," Sebastian whispered. "The two of you can't eye-fuck, or this won't work. The last thing we need is to have pictures of that all over social media, saying that Scotlin May's fiancé is having an affair."

I took the glass he was holding out to me, taking my eyes off King, which was hard to do. All I wanted to do was look at him. No, that wasn't true. I wanted to be on his arm. As close to him as I could get.

"What happens when the engagement ends?" I asked him.

Sebastian took a drink of his whiskey. "The stalker will be caught then. Because it's a political thing, we won't be handling the man. He'll be handed over to the authorities. Scotlin will break off the engagement because of the trauma and move to Paris for some emotional recovery. Jefferson will be the protective father who stands by her and demands justice. It'll all turn out nicely for them in the public eye. If her abortion ever becomes public knowledge, the hopes are it will be overshadowed by this. Once he's in office and the stalker is set free, he will … disappear."

I took a drink of my water, then asked, "Disappear?"

He nodded once.

"Meaning?"

Sebastian looked down at me. "Meaning we'll handle him then."

Oh. Ohhh. "I see."

I scanned the crowd and the people arriving, using all my restraint not to look at King. It wasn't an easy task. I was so very tempted.

"Do you think the man is here?" I asked Sebastian.

He started to speak when a smile was suddenly on his face, and his attention was focused on an older gentleman with a black cowboy hat covering most of his white hair. His short, trimmed beard was equally white. He was shorter than Sebastian by several inches, but the way he stood gave an air of authority.

"You're looking more like your father every day," the man said, shaking Sebastian's hand. "More so than that brother of yours."

Sebastian chuckled. "I'm sure Thatcher would take that as a compliment," he replied, then turned to me. "Rumor, this is Dawson Woodrow. Dawson, this is Rumor Beauregard. She's a close friend of the family."

The older gentleman gave me a nod and tipped his hat at me. "Nice to meet you, Miss Beauregard. I've been buying winning racehorses from the Shephards for nigh on thirty years."

"They do have the best, but please, call me Rumor."

He gave me an appreciative look, then cut his eyes to Sebastian. "I'd hang on to this one."

Sebastian laughed, but I could see him glance over in King's direction. When he responded, he turned the subject around to the Derby, and I only half listened as they discussed the horses that had raced. My eyes scanned the room, finding those I recognized, which were all family members. Ronan Salazar and Jupiter were to the far right of the room, speaking with guests. I could see Ronan casually glancing over in King's direction, as if he was watching him. Making sure he didn't leave his post.

As close as I was to Maeme, I barely knew Ronan or Jupiter. I adored their daughter, Birdie, but I wondered if the baby would bring them around more. Would I ever really feel like they were my family? They would be my child's grandparents. King never spoke of his mother, and I wondered if she would want to know the baby. We hadn't ever discussed it, but I wanted my baby to have all the family she could. Something I never had. To grow up loved and adored. The more family, the better.

· THIRTY-TWO ·

He broke my fucking nose!

KING

I wasn't going to last much longer. Every fucking cocksucker who looked at her with even a mere glance, I wanted to rip out their heart. Sebastian was obeying. He hadn't come close to touching her again. This was a level of hell I hadn't known existed, and although I knew I belonged in hell, I wasn't dead yet.

"You need to stop watching her like she's your next meal," Scotlin hissed between her teeth as she smiled.

"She is my next meal," I replied. "As soon as this bullshit is over."

"Ugh, King. TMI," she said, sounding disgusted.

What-the-fuck-ever. She had no idea how sweet Rumor's pussy was.

"You look like you're about to face a lifetime sentence. At least try and smile."

"This is the best I can do," I replied.

"Look, I'm as ready for this to be over as you are. I thought it would be more fun, but I hadn't been aware you'd become … this."

Rumor laughed at something Luella, Roland's wife, said, and my chest tightened. I wanted to be close enough to hear that sound.

I'd upset her when she got here, and it had taken a while for her to relax again. It wasn't like I could help it. She'd arrived, touching Sebastian and looking like an angel.

My angel.

"All the guests have arrived," Jefferson informed us. "Scotlin, go with your mother to mingle with the guests. King, I need a word with you."

I didn't want to leave the room. That meant I couldn't see Rumor. I tore my eyes off her to look at him. "Now?"

He nodded.

"Can it not wait until this is over? I should be here if anything out of place happens." Meaning so I could protect Rumor and get her the fuck out.

"The room is well secured," he replied. "This can't wait."

I looked at Sebastian, willing him to meet my gaze. He was too engrossed in a conversation with one of Scotlin's cousins to notice. Fuck. I'd be quick. She was fine. Right now, she had Sebastian at her side, and Storm was only a few feet away.

"Okay," I clipped, turning to follow him from the ballroom.

He continued walking until we reached the study, then opened the door, stepping back for me to enter before closing it behind us. For his sake, I hoped he wasn't about to correct me for watching Rumor. I didn't give a flying fuck who he was. I'd watch her if I wanted to. She was mine. No one was telling me otherwise.

"How do you know this Rumor Beauregard?"

My jaw clenched. "She's mine."

His eyes widened. "I see. But where did she come from? She's not from our circle."

"Why?" I bit out, deciding on how I could kill the next governor of Georgia and hide it.

His eyes narrowed. "I have my sources, King. I can very easily go get your father and ask him these questions. I chose you as a sign of respect since it was very clear she belonged to you. You've yet to stop watching her since she arrived."

Count to fucking ten. Don't break the man's neck.

"Rumor was brought to Maeme's and kept under our protection. I don't see how this affects you at all."

"She's not from Georgia then?" he asked.

I shook my head. I'd walk out of here if the man's interest in what was mine didn't raise the hairs on my neck. She shouldn't be on his radar, and I would be damned if he started asking around about her.

"You can either tell me about her or I can have a background check done. I have my reasons for asking these questions."

"Because I am engaged to your daughter for the moment? That's not a reason, Jefferson. That's you poking your nose where it doesn't belong. Our job is to get Scotlin's stalker. Protect you and your family's name and make sure you are the next governor. That is where it ends. You aren't family. Rumor is."

The shocked expression on his face at the last part annoyed me. This entire fucking situation was pissing me off.

"She's family now?"

"Yes," I snarled, unable to control the rage he'd ignited inside my chest.

"I see. That makes this even more of an issue. I need to know where she came from."

"No."

"Why can't you tell me that? Wouldn't you rather I come to you than go to Stellan or your father?"

I took a step in his direction, wanting to wrap my hands around his neck. He must have read that clearly in my expression, but he only tensed up. He didn't back away. Fucker knew I couldn't kill him, no matter how badly I wanted to.

"What is it you want to know?" I demanded.

"Did you find her in Louisiana?" he asked.

He knew something. I didn't like it. He was holding something from me about her, and I was close to snapping right here in this goddamn room. He was going to need backup when I did.

"No. But she was born there."

His face paled, and he took in a deep breath. "What part?"

"You need to get to the fucking point, May. My patience is almost gone, and I can't promise you that I will be able to control what happens next."

"Her last name. It isn't really Beauregard, is it?"

I thought for a moment, then decided I might as well give him what he needed to know if I was going to get to the bottom of this. I shook my head. "It's LeBlanc."

Jefferson backed up two steps, then sank down onto the chair behind him. "Fuck," he whispered.

"You're gonna need to say more than that," I demanded, not liking this at all.

We'd had a complete background check done on Rumor before I ever laid eyes on her. I knew her story. Her past. There was nothing of concern other than she'd suffered a lot and I was still hunting down the bastard who had hurt her when she was younger.

"I knew her mother," he said, staring at the floor. "When she walked in the house and I saw her, it was like I'd been thrown back in time. She's a complete replica. Even the hair. For a moment, I thought ... it was her. But then I realized that was impossible."

I felt as if he'd just hurled a brick into my chest. "She doesn't know her mother. She grew up in the foster system."

He closed his eyes for a moment and whispered what fucking looked like, "Thank God."

What the hell was that about? Her life had been a nightmare, and he was thanking God for it. Son of a bitch was stepping too far out of line.

"You got five motherfucking seconds to explain yourself," I warned him.

"Ariella LeBlanc is the only skeleton I have in my closet. I've never come close to it being aired in my career. I've lost sleep over the fact that she'd come forward. Someone would find her and offer her money to talk," he said, then lifted his eyes to meet my glare. "I met her on a business trip. She worked at a club I frequented. One look at her, and, well, I was hooked. It went on for six months, and then one day, she told me she was pregnant. I wrote her a check for half a million and told her to get an abortion and the rest was hush money. I never went back. Ten years later, I did send out some feelers when my political career was taking off. I wanted to make sure that door was closed tight. There was no sign of her. Not a trace."

There were several things running through my head as he spoke, but the one thing that trumped them all.

"How many years ago?" I demanded, my hands shaking at my sides. I fisted them, but the tremors of the unleashed wrath expanding with every breath I took didn't ease.

"Almost twenty-five," he replied.

I exploded with a loud roar as I charged him, grabbing his shirt and throwing him back against the wall. The monster in my chest had torn me wide open and stepped out to take control. I wanted to rip him limb from limb. See him beg for mercy. Bleed out at my feet while I watched the life dim from his eyes until he was a bloody corpse.

A loud sound came from behind me, but I didn't care. Nothing mattered. This bastard had paid for Rumor to be aborted. MY RUMOR. He'd wanted to kill her before she was born. I felt hands on my arms pulling at me, but I jerked free as an animalistic sound tore from my throat. He was going to die.

"KING!"

I heard my name, but it barely registered. They could hang me on a cross for this, but I would end this man.

Arms wrapped around my chest and arms, pulling me back. I fought, snarling and cursing, but I couldn't break free.

"YOU ARE A DEAD MAN!" I told him.

His eyes were wide, and his face was as white as the shirt he was wearing.

"What the fuck, King?" Storm was close to my ear.

I threw my head back and a loud, "FUCK!" followed it as the hands around my chest eased up almost enough for me to break free.

"A little help here?" Wells said on my other side.

"He broke my fucking nose! I'm doing all I can!"

That was Sebastian. Why was he here? Who was with Rumor?

"Rumor!" I demanded, turning frantically toward the door.

"She's with Maeme and Stellan. Thatcher is in there, too, keeping his eyes on everyone. Not to mention, she's got a goddamn illegal Taser Maeme put in her purse," Sebastian said.

"Someone needs to start explaining what the hell is going on in here," Monte said, slamming the door behind him as he walked inside. His eyes swung to Jefferson's and back to me. "Did you attack Jefferson?" he asked incredulously.

"When I get free of these three, I'm gonna fucking kill him," I replied, seething as I stared at the man who had given the woman I worshipped life, but had left her to be killed. Paid for it. She'd lived a goddamn nightmare, growing up, while he spoiled that bitch daughter of his and gave her everything she wanted.

"Stop!" Storm barked at me. "We aren't letting you kill Jefferson. Calm the fuck down."

"Someone needs to start explaining," Barrett demanded.

I hadn't even realized he was in here too.

I didn't take my eyes off the bastard still pressed against the wall, watching me like I was a madman. He had no idea how fucking insane I was. But he would. When these fuckers let me go.

"I …" he started, swallowing hard. "I recognized Rumor. Or someone who is identical to her. She … I knew her mother once. I wanted to verify that she was who I thought she was. I didn't realize it was going to set him off. I was going to him about it out of respect since it was clear she, uh … was his. I didn't know he'd react like this, or I would have spoken to Stellan."

"You tried to have her aborted, you piece of fucking trash!" I shouted as the others held on to me tightly. They couldn't hold me forever.

"Fucking hell," Monte said, walking over to sit down where Jefferson had been earlier.

"Are you saying you knew Rumor's mother?" Barrett asked.

"YES, he fucking knew her. He used her, then walked away. Left her money to abort the kid he'd made and never looked back," I said as my entire body shook.

I had never hated anyone as much as I did this man. Well, except for Churchill Millroe. They were tied for first.

"Shit," Storm muttered, his grip on my left arm tightening. "We need to get him out of here. He's not going to shake this off anytime soon."

"Go. We will deal with the rest."

"This isn't over," I warned Jefferson.

They pushed me until I moved toward the door. It opened before we reached it, and Thatcher walked inside. His eyes went to me being held to scope out the rest of the room.

"What did I miss?" he asked.

"Just help us get him out of this fucking house before he begins tearing it and everyone in his path to shreds," Storm told him.

Thatcher smirked. "That sounds like a good time. You sure you don't want to let him go?"

"Go get your father," Monte said to him. "And … you probably need to get Rumor too. She might be all that calms him down."

Thatcher glanced at me one more time, raising his eyebrows, as if he was simply entertained, then turned to leave.

"You act like this around Rumor, and she's gonna be fucking terrified," Sebastian told me.

I didn't respond as they ushered me from the house and out toward one of the limos parked out front.

"If we let you go, are you going to stay still and wait on Rumor?"

I stared up at the house, knowing I couldn't go in there and murder the goddamn state representative.

"Yes," I said through clenched teeth.

Storm let go first, but the other two didn't seem to trust me. Wells eased back as if he was more worried about me turning on him. Sebastian followed him, and I shook my arms out and stalked over to grip the roof of the limo and brace myself. I had to clear my head. Not think about it. If I let myself think about it, I'd lose it again.

"You good? Because here she comes," Storm told me.

I turned back around as Thatcher walked down the stairs with Rumor at his side. The shimmering green dress she wore clung to her every curve and hit way too fucking high on her legs for my liking. She was the most stunning creature I'd ever laid my eyes on, and the man who was supposed to protect her, give her a home, cherish her had paid her mother to kill her. Before she was ever given a chance at life.

But her mother hadn't done it. And she was alive and perfect. Walking toward me with that sweet angelic face etched with concern. For me.

How the hell had I gotten this lucky?

Unable to wait any longer, I went to her, grabbing her by the waist and taking her mouth. I needed to be reminded she was mine. She was here with me. The past hadn't happened the way Jefferson May had planned. Her life had been shit because of his neglect, but I'd be sure the rest of it was a motherfucking fairy tale.

Her hands went to my chest and fisted in my shirt as she leaned into me, wanting more. I was about to give her more. So much more that she was going to be begging me to give her a moment to catch her breath.

"Get her in the limo," Thatcher drawled, interrupting us. "Last thing everyone needs to see is you sucking her face off when this is your engagement party to Scotlin."

Pulling back, I looked into her eyes and reassured myself that she was fine. I had her now, and all the bad was over. Never again would she live through it.

"What's wrong?" she asked me, reaching up to touch my face.

I leaned into her soft hand. "Nothing now."

"He's one of those psychos disguised with a pretty face. He seems charming and shit until you flip the wrong trigger," Thatcher said casually.

She frowned, turning to look at him with a scowl marring her forehead. "He is not a psycho," she informed him. "Don't talk about him like that."

I heard a laugh, smothered with a cough, behind me.

"Come on, sweets. Let's go home."

She looked back at me. "But the party. You can't leave yet."

"The fuck he can't," Storm said. "Y'all get in, and please, Rumor, keep his ass busy all night."

She glanced past me to Storm. "What happened? I missed something."

I wasn't sure if I would be able to tell her the truth about Jefferson May. I knew I had to, but when I did, I couldn't be sure her reaction wouldn't send me to the man's doorstep, ready to slit his goddamn throat again.

"A lot," I said. "The only thing you need to know right now is, the fake engagement is over."

"It is?"

The hopefulness in her voice sliced through me. She'd put up with this shit, and I knew it had been hard on her. No more. Never again.

"Yeah, sweets, it is."

"No one believed it anyway." Wells spoke up. "The way he was watching you all night, it was clear who he wanted."

The smile that curled her face made me chuckle. My girl liked that. She paused, and then her eyes went wide in shock.

"Sebastian!" she said, pressing a hand to her chest. "What happened to your face!"

I hadn't paid any attention to him earlier, but now looking at the blood on his face and on the front of his shirt, I should have probably had him go somewhere else before she saw him.

His eyes swung to me. He wasn't about to tell her I had done it.

"He ran into the back of King's head," Storm said, then pointed at the open door of the limo, wanting us gone.

"How did you do that?" she asked him as we reached the limo.

"Accident. He's clumsy as fuck," I told her, then placed a hand on her ass to keep her dress down while nudging her to get inside.

I looked back at him. "I'd say we're even now."

"For what?" Wells asked.

"For touching Rumor," Storm explained.

I knew she had heard him when her head swung around to look at me in horror.

Grinning, I climbed inside as Storm closed the door behind me.

"What, sweets? I can't help it if he ran into my head."

She narrowed her eyes. "You're not telling me the truth. He barely touched my elbow, King."

"Don't care," I told her, pulling up her dress and sliding my hand between her thighs. "And you won't either in about five seconds."

She opened her mouth to argue, but the moment I slid my finger inside of her panties, she let out a gasp instead and spread her legs open like the good girl she was.

· THIRTY-THREE ·

That's it. Scream. I want people to hear you.

RUMOR

There had once been a time when I would have given anything to know my father. I had fantasized about it for so many years. What he looked like. What he would say when he found me. Unfortunately, none of those daydreams had turned out to be reality.

Jefferson May was very likely the man whose sperm had helped create me, but he was and would never be anything more. Having the truth about my conception, the two people who had given me life, it changed nothing really. It didn't destroy me. Other than a small pang of what I would never have, it affected me very little.

I didn't need parents. I had Maeme. I didn't need a father who loved and adored me. I had a man who met all my needs. King was everything to me. All the love in the world couldn't compare to the way he made me feel. He cherished me, and every time I caught him looking at me as if I were the only light in his life, I knew that I had found my home.

King was my home. He was better than anything I could have imagined or even hoped for. I was complete.

I placed a hand on the small bump underneath my shirt. We were complete. The life inside of me was a part of us, and she would never know a life where her father didn't adore her and her mother didn't love her unconditionally.

Strong arms came around me, and King's much larger hands covered mine. I laid my head back on his chest and sighed with contentment. We had moved into his house two months ago, shortly after the engagement party.

King had refused to continue the fake engagement, and thankfully, after Blaise Hughes heard about what had happened, he agreed that they had to go another route. King could no longer be allowed near Jefferson. I'd feared Blaise's reaction, but King had said that he understood.

Today, we were going to paint the nursery pink. My intuition had been right. We were having a little girl. I still wished I had a photo of King's face when Dr. Drew told us. He'd looked lost and terrified, all at once. He had thought it was a boy. In his mind, a boy was something durable and tough. He saw a girl as someone fragile. I had a lot to teach him about that, clearly.

"What are you standing out here thinking about?" he asked against my ear.

"Us. Our life. Picturing the swing set she will have one day, over there by the oak tree," I replied.

I had always wanted a swing set with a playhouse attached.

King nuzzled my ear. "That's funny."

I tilted my head back to look up at him. "What is?"

He pressed a kiss to my nose. "That you were thinking about swing sets while I was thinking about bending you over the rail and fucking you from behind."

A laugh bubbled out of me. "I might be convinced."

He pressed another kiss to my lips. "Tell me what I need to do, and I will."

I turned around until I was facing him and pushed down my shorts. "Use your imagination," I replied.

His eyes dropped to my legs, and then he reached between them, running a finger over my slit. "You sure you were thinking about swing sets, sweets? This pussy is soaking wet."

I sucked in some air and nodded. "Yeah, but lately, I stay wet and achy."

His eyes flared. "Achy? As in you need to come?"

I nodded.

"It feels different," he said, lowering himself to his knees and pushing my legs open so he could inspect me. He slid his knuckles through my open lips. "It looks swollen," he murmured, then leaned in to lick, causing my knees to buckle.

"Mmm, I'm gonna need to eat it first," he said, grabbing the chair closest to him and pushing me down into it. "Can't have you collapsing on me." He took my right leg and put it over the arm of the chair. "Damn, that's pretty."

I watched as he slid his hands under my bottom and pulled me to him before burying his face there and humming with pleasure as his tongue took long, slow strokes.

I slid my fingers into his hair and arched up to meet his mouth. He squeezed and pressed me in closer, growling as he did it.

"King," I panted, my head falling back on the chair.

"That's my sweet girl. I want your cum all over my face. So I can smell you all day."

His naughty talk always sped things up.

I pulled at his hair and cried out, knowing that I was about to come. It gripped me, and I felt the gush as he let out a hungry groan just as my body splintered into a million brilliant, orgasmic pulses.

King licked my thighs as if he didn't want to miss a drop before taking my hand and jerking me out of the chair, then spinning me around. His hand slapped my ass hard, causing me to jump. "That's my fucking good girl," he snarled as he slapped the other side.

"Opening for me. So sweet. Now, you're gonna squeeze my cock and take my load."

I moaned and nodded.

He slammed into me hard, causing the chair to scrape against the deck. I cried out, gripping on to it to keep from falling.

"That's it. Scream. I want people to hear you. Know I own this pussy. I'm the one filling it up." He wrapped my hair around his hand and pulled back, causing my back to bend, then took my mouth hard.

I could taste myself, and it made me tremble from the dirtiness of it and how much I liked it.

"It's fucking sweet, isn't it?" he said as he thrust inside of me.

I felt another orgasm coming and let out a low moan just as he jerked behind me. I met his thrusts, wanting it as wild and unhinged as he could give it. Dark, dirty, twisted words fell from his mouth as our bodies slapped against each other.

When the climax took me, I shouted his name, and his arms wrapped around me as his release shot inside of me.

We'd had sex in most rooms of the house, but this was a first for the back patio. Smiling, I fell forward, resting my head on my hands, which were still holding on to the chair.

He moved away from me, but I didn't move—I knew not to. He wanted to see it. He always wanted to see it. I shivered as his fingers played with his cum leaking from me, and he shoved it back inside me. Turning my head, I opened my mouth obediently, and he slid those same fingers into my mouth for me to suck.

"Almost fucking perfect." His voice was thick.

Almost?

He removed his fingers from between my lips, and I let them go. Then, he tugged his jeans back up before reaching into his pocket. I glanced up at his face, confused, as I turned to sit down on the chair, about to ask him about that *almost* comment.

Before I did, he lowered himself to one knee and took my hand.

I saw it then.

The diamond ring glittering in the sunlight. I sucked in a breath as he picked up my hand and slid it onto my finger. He lifted his eyes to look at me with a wicked smile on his handsome face. Taking my hand, he kissed my ring finger.

"Now, it's perfect."

Coming May 22, 2024
SIZZLING book three in the Georgia Smoke Series

Get ready for Storm Kingston

· ABOUT ABBI ·

Abbi Glines is a #1 New York Times, USA Today, Wall Street Journal, and International bestselling author of the Rosemary Beach, Sea Breeze, Smoke Series, Vincent Boys, Boys South of the Mason Dixon, and The Field Party Series. She is also author to the Sweet Trilogy and the Black Souls Trilogy. She believes in ghosts and has a habit of asking people if their house is haunted before she goes in it. Her house was built in 1820 and she finally has her own haunted house but they're friendly spirits. She drinks afternoon tea because she wants to be British but alas she was born in Alabama although she now lives in New England (which makes her feel a little closer to the British). When asked how many books she has written she has to stop and count on her fingers and even then she still forgets a few. When she's not locked away writing, she is entertaining her first grade daughter, she is reading (if everyone in her house including the ghosts will leave her alone long enough), shopping online (major Amazon Prime addiction), and planning her next Disney World vacation (and now that her oldest daughter Annabelle works at Disney she has an excuse to frequent it often).

You can connect with Abbi online in several different ways. She uses social media to procrastinate.

Facebook: AbbiGlinesAuthor
Twitter: abbiglines
Instagram: abbiglines
Snapchat: abbiglines
TikTok: abbiglines

Printed in Dunstable, United Kingdom